Prisoners of Our Own Device

By Jane Dee Simpson

Contents

Acknowledgements

Firstly, I wish to thank my agent Emerantia Parnall-Gilbert for her faith in me from the outset when presented with a synopsis and an unformatted mini manuscript. Thank you Emerantia for your friendship and advice given to a complete technophobe to turn what you were given into a finished manuscript. s

The Tate Gallery is, of course, a real gallery and I am certain that its ethics are not those portrayed in the story, so I apologize for this artistic license. Jian Arts Limited did exist and did have a covenant with the Republic of China, to contribute to the Wolong Panda Reserve from the sale of its porcelain Panda figurines. For the sake of the story, I have changed dates etcetera for which I hope I am forgiven especially by Makoto Azuma who did work on the flower etched bottles originally designed by Emile Galles for Perrier Jouet, but it was much later than the millennium year.

To add authenticity, I have used the names of some very real esteemed art collectors and critics though no words have been ascribed to them in the story.

Dedication

I dedicate this book to my friend Jane who has supported me, fed, watered and listened to me throughout the lengthy process of my endeavors to write this book. Many thanks.

"We are all prisoners here, of our own device"

The Eagles, Hotel California

Stone walls do not a prison make,

Nor iron bars a cage;

Minds innocent and quiet take

That for an hermitage;

If I have freedom in my love,

And in my soul am free,

Angels alone that soar above

Enjoy such liberty.

Richard Lovelace 1618 - 1657

PART ONE

Chapter One

Thwack, the ball smashed into the racquet, the sound reverberated around the court, a host of heads turned synonymously following its course. A puff of chalk stirred the still mid-afternoon air as the ball bounced alongside the farthest white line. Agafina Mihailovna punched the air with her clenched fist and mouthed the word "Yes" through clenched teeth.

"Advantage Miss Mihailovna."

Mihailovna steadied herself, nailing her opponent with a steely stare as she skipped to and fro on the backline of the court. She bounced her chosen ball four times her obsessive little quirk, swayed backward onto her heels, and almost lazily tossed the ball into the air. Thwack, she rushed the net, braking sharply her Nike tennis shoes raising a little dust where the court was worn, the tension in her muscles taut, then relaxed and smiled with satisfaction as the ball touched on the left of the center line and crashed resoundingly into the far barrier unhindered.

"Game Miss Mihailovna. Miss Mihailovna leads five games to four. First set."

Both players walked to their respective chairs at the side of the court. Mihailovna took the towel from the ball girl and proceeded to wipe the handle of her racquet, casually scanning the crowd seated immediately in front of her, when her gaze was riveted, jarred, by the penetrating glance of a pair of arctic blue eyes. A small shudder crept along her spine. The sunlight glinted on a mane of white-blonde hair, turning its' wayward strands to spun silver as the slight breeze teased it. Mihailovna took the proffered drink and sipped slowly as her eyes swept over the face, down the graceful curve of the throat and came to rest on the deep shadow between the golden orbs of the woman's breasts. A slight lopsided smile played about her lips as the nipples began to rise and swell beneath the damp thin silk of the woman's chemise. Shifting her gaze back, she raised her eyebrows questioningly as a slight flush spread across the woman's high cheekbones and the lips parted emitting a small audible gasp.

Shit thought Mihailovna as the umpire announced, "Time ladies please."

Chapter Two

When the light had faded and the tennis was over for the day, Ella Michaels had paid a visit to the large detached art deco villa on the Esplanade, where her company, Marbelous Jae's, had been contracted to do the interior design and decoration. She rarely involved herself with the work these days, but since this job had come up in Eastbourne she had arranged to be there to oversee the work and use the opportunity to take in the pre-Wimbledon ladies tennis tournament at the same time. Other than equestrian events tennis was the only sport that she took an interest in.

During the past five years, she'd had little leisure time to spend but the Wimbledon Tournament especially had become her one indulgence and the pre-Wimbledon ladies tournament at Eastbourne was a great precursor. Since her second divorce, and second failure, in Ella's mind she had started her own interior design business, doing specialized paintwork, frescos, marbling, rag rolling etcetera and had been 'hands-on' from the beginning. As the demand for her work increased Ella had asked a couple of friends, who were in dead-end jobs, to join her as partners and Marbelous Jae's had been the result. Ella Michael's style and attention to detail had served to make all three relatively wealthy women.

Ella, Joy, and Ao had been good friends for many years. Joy was a small dark bubble of laughter; she and Ella shared a mutual sense of the ridiculous. Ao, a tall willowy, nubile princess of the Nile, had studied interior design and was Joy's lover. Joy's main ambition was to be a singer comedienne. She had used the money they had made wisely, writing songs, making demo discs and now that she was main spotting in many venues and guesting on quite a few TV comedy shows she rarely took any part in the company; only Ao remained to run the business with a little help from Ella and a select team of talented though quite often unqualified helpers

Ella's real love was to sculpt in clay, something she had started doing whilst living in Spain for a few years with John her last husband and her children. She found she had a talent for it, had built a new company, manufacturing fine art porcelain limited editions which were sold by direct mail order. Jian Arts Limited had made a considerable fortune in the first year of trading by cutting out the middle man; selling limited editions of Ella's work fine pieces of art in themselves but now more affordable to the general public and had gone on to make Ella an extremely wealthy woman in her own right.

With Jian selling its products worldwide Ella had finally been able to indulge her emerging passions and for the past two years had been working steadily preparing for her first-ever exhibition, six major bronzes on a theme entitled Prisoners.

After checking all was well on-site at the job, Ella returned to her hotel The Grand in Eastbourne. Parking her yellow open-top Toyota Supra in the hotel car park, she lit a cigarette inhaled deeply and allowed her mind to wander over the events of the day.

Chapter Three

Mihailovna had unnerved her, she hadn't seriously thought about sex for a couple of years, preferring the more painless uncomplicated celibacy of her present lifestyle. Relationships didn't seem to work for Ella. Both her ex-husbands had complained that they couldn't get close enough to her, that she didn't give anything back into the exchange. They were right of course, she supposed, she had held herself back, anticipating their betrayal and in the end, they had proven her right. Sculpture had become her life now and had proved a catheter to her emotions. Pushing the boundaries of her work drained her, she injected such depth of feeling into each individual piece that there was little to spare, to spend on demonstrations of affection, petty jealousies or even family crises and she had had her fair share of those over the years. She could not afford to worry about a partner's infidelities, or nurture their fragile egos and had kept herself free of involvement for the past two years.

The best thing to come from either marriage had been her children Crystal and Jasper. She had loved them unquestioningly, and each family crisis every little bit of teenage angst had been costly to her work, but they were grown now and she was as free as she would ever be and had made a pact with herself not to become involved in any relationships, allowing nothing to disturb her frame of mind.

At this moment though, she was rattled. Her mind slid backward, turning inside herself to a place deep within. She tried to bury the memories but somehow they always crept up on her, insidiously, like smoke beneath a closed but unsealed door.

Chapter Four

Ella had been born in Manchester, the seventh child of Chaim

Mickiewicz and Elizabeth Jane Carey, and named Gabriella, though

not christened since both were practicing communists. Ella's father,

a Polish Jew, had been a member of the Special Forces during World

War 11 and had been amongst the first people to enter the Nazi

Concentration Camps of Auschwitz and Dachau. What he had been

confronted with there, such unspeakable evil had defied

comprehension.

After the war, Chaim became a changed man unable to divorce

himself from the horrors he had witnessed, no longer the proud loving

father his family had known. He had begun to drink heavily, the

alcohol an accelerant which plunged him deeper into his paranoid

nightmares and when he came home to Elizabeth drunk, the fights

and beatings would start and Elizabeth would make excuses for the

ensuing bruises. It was as though he blamed his wife, blamed her for not keeping his faith, for losing his orthodox family, it appeared he blamed her for his very survival. In his tortured mind the difference between her Irish Catholic heritage and his Jewish one that while they both wallowed in guilt she could seek absolution whilst he never could. He had seen Jews go to the gas chambers blaming themselves for everything bad that happened to them. He never worked again but became steeped in the alcoholic mists of his misery and guilt and plunged them all into abject poverty.

Ella's first memories were of the noise of screaming and shouting, broken glass and crockery littering the floor and her mother's tenseness, her panic infecting all the children as the pub's closing time drew near. Elizabeth Mickiewicz was Roman Catholic by birth and whilst not a practicing one still adhered to the sanctity of the marriage vows. It took much soul searching and the repeated exhortations of friends but she finally plucked up the courage to leave her husband and file for divorce, social suicide in the post-war era, effectively cutting her off forever from any family help and so she struggled taking in washing and ironing in an age without the convenience of steam irons and automatic washing machines. Ella remembered the hiss and the smell as her mother skimmed the cast iron over a bar of soap to make it run smoother. She also held down two jobs as a daily cleaning woman, her once lovely hands becoming withered weathered and worn the skin red from the bleach and her fingernails were broken and torn.

Ella had been five years old when her parents separated and for a few months, a semblance of peace descended on the family before the only son, seventeen years old Stephan took up his father's mantle and imposed his own rules enforced by his own brand of brutality. Stephan had an enormous IQ and was himself a good draftsman and watercolor artist but had been forced to seek work without qualifications in order to provide support for his six sisters and became a misogynist, a true woman-hater who never married and in later life, his resentment developed into obsessive-compulsive disorder and he became increasingly eccentric.

Gabriella Mickiewicz had lived inside her own mind, played solitary games with cut out paper people, and allowed her imagination to carry her away from the fear and pain, away from the violence and noise of constant arguments and the habitual ugliness of poverty, escaping in her mind what she couldn't escape physically, and lived only for the beauty she could create with her drawings and her vivid dreamlike imaginings. She read from an early age and books became her 'passport' to other worlds, fuelled her dreams and added credence to her creativity. Gabriella felt no kinship with her family, Elizabeth was a good mother, but distant, Gabriella had no memories of the comfort of her mother's arms and often daydreamed that she was a changeling or an adopted child but logic prevailed and she knew deep inside what she saw as the terrible reality of her genetic inheritance ran through her veins.

She was always aware that what she had witnessed with her siblings and the physical abuse she suffered in her childhood could mean that the same propensity for anger and violence lurked deep within the dark side of her psyche. She was afraid of the depths of her own passions, afraid that if she opened Pandora's Box the tightly wound substance of her self would spiral, unravel and descend into the violence and insanity which she felt infected her life.

Ella thought that once that ugliness had been forced into you it became part of the blood that coursed through your veins, diluting it and staining every part of your body, the ugliness never coming out but growing and spreading like malevolent cancer. She hoped to control it, force it into a tight ball in a tight place and keep it there, locked down.

Chapter Five

This is ridiculous Ella thought, gays had never bothered her before. Joy and Ao her business partners were lovers and great friends, she had shared flats with gays, wined and dined among them, even been out on the razzle a few times with them. Pippa Adams, the former British tennis champion also a celebrated lesbian had been a close friend for some two years. Ella had decorated Pippa's home and whilst working there, Pippa had made a pass at Ella, more than a pass really, but though they had kissed a few times had, in fact, slept together, sleep was all that it had been and it had been more to do with the wine and the grass they had been smoking than any real attraction, at least on Ella's side.

Pippa was a collector of fine arts, was on the board of the Tate Gallery and this was what sustained the friendship. It had been Pippa's insistence, which had brought about the forthcoming exhibition of Ella's work, at the Tate Gallery.

Ella entered the air-conditioned coolness of The Grand's hotel foyer and waited to collect her key from the receptionist. Mihailovna had followed her in with several other players and commentators from the tournament, amongst them Pippa Adams. Pippa called to Ella as she was heading for the lifts.

"Ella, how about we do dinner together later, we have some things to discuss".

Ella turned and smiled in Pippa's direction, "Sure, I'm in room 520, call me later, okay."

Mihailovna almost did a double-take, did Pippa Adams know the woman she had been flirting with, and then again, could the woman possibly be gay? There was certainly something about this woman, whoever she was. Mihailovna honed in on Pippa Adams. She laid a gently restraining hand on Pippa's arm, "Pippa darling, lovely to see you, come, join me for a cold drink." Mihailovna had the very slightest of accents, almost overridden by an American one.

"What do you want Gaffy? You rarely make a beeline for me unless you want something in particular."

"Moi! Would I do that?" said Mihailovna laughing and steering Pippa across the plush cerise carpeting to the privacy of the Georgian pillared gallery with its' high ornately molded ceiling and small baroque tables for two. The gallery looked out of large heavily draped windows to the sea sparkling in the remains of the early evening sunlight.

"Who's your friend, new lady? Quite something, definitely a looker."

"Ella? She's a friend that's all. She's an artist actually, a sculptor to be precise. She's having an exhibition soon at the Tate and since I'm on the board there we have a few things to iron out together."

"Is she any good?"

"No, she's not just good, she's bloody brilliant. She really has the most remarkable talent I've ever seen."

Mihailovna raised her eyebrows and adopted an almost camp delivery "A sculptor, eh! I've often thought of having a sculpture done of myself. Does she do that, you know___commissions of people?" She gestured with her hands as she talked a European euphemism she had not lost with Americanization.

"Yes, as far as I know, but you'd have to sit for her and when would you have time?"

"Hey when this is over here I have a couple of practice weeks before Wimbledon and then there's after of course. This will be my tenth title if I win and then well, I'm thinking of going out on a good note. A sculpture would be a good way of marking the end of my career, don't you think? Perhaps you could mention it to her, just say I'm thinking of having something done and why doesn't she do it. I would pay well of course and I'm sure there would be prestige involved, I am the world No.1 after all."

"I'll mention it to her though this is one time your money or fame isn't going to talk for you, she doesn't need it."

Sadly for me, Pippa thought.

"She's already got everything she wants in her life. She's probably the most altogether person I've ever met. The only person I've ever met who seems to exist totally within themselves, she seems unconcerned with the peripheries of life that worry the rest of us."

Chapter Six

Pippa replaced the receiver of the phone at her bedside cabinet after arranging to meet Ella downstairs.

Ella, ahhh___! Ella, she thought sighing, if only, but then Michaels had little room in her life for anyone other than her immediate family and a couple of close friends.

Pippa thought back to when they had first met. She had wanted her house in Berkshire decorating and not looking forward to the ensuing mess and paint fumes she thought it best to happen while she was commentating on an international tournament and had intended to spend some time with Lisa, her current lover, afterward, but things had gone wrong between them and she had returned early, alone and somewhat disconsolate.

Arriving home late that evening, soaking wet from the storm raging outside she had shaken out her wet hair bemoaning the fact that it would most likely frizz, kicked off her shoes and left her coat dripping pools of water onto the marble tiles of the spacious hallway. She had been surprised to discovered lights still blazing and music drifting from the sitting room then remembered at the last moment that it was probably the decorators still working.

Entering quietly into the room she was assaulted by a vision of loveliness. There she was, Ella Micheals a barely dressed woman, loose black vest, and baggy shorts, covered in splashes and odd brushstrokes of paint, surgeon's gloves on her hands, their creaminess offset against the golden tan of her skin, and a baseball cap on her head, she appeared to be painting Pippa's wall with a large white goose feather pausing to consider the effects of her work then adding a touch more here and there. The music blasting from an iPod was Enigma's 'Mia Culpa' she was totally absorbed by its Gregorian chanting and throbbing beat, swaying with the rhythm, completely unaware of Pippa's entrance. Pippa couldn't see her face but her body was superb, tanned, graceful in movement, not an athlete's physique, long muscled, more like a swimmer. The storm raged on outside, white-hot lightning filled the room and yet she remained completely oblivious, content in her own world.

As though sensing another's presence Ella had turned suddenly and looked directly into Pippa's eyes.

"Hello, you're back early. Well, really I've finished here. If you'll just give me a short while I'll clear most of this debris away into the garage and my people will collect it tomorrow sometime".

"There's no rush, the weather's terrible outside and I can't quite see you leaving dressed like that."

"Oh! No," Ella laughed, "I have some other clothes with me, I did intend to take a shower and change but it doesn't matter."

"No, please go ahead; in fact, the company would be great right now if you'd like to ride out the storm. I could open a bottle of Chablis and find something to eat."

"No I couldn't impose, and anyway I have my car here and I have to drive to the hotel so it wouldn't be wise to drink. But thanks anyway for the offer, though I will take you up on the shower if you really don't mind."

Ella peeled off the latex gloves and removed the baseball cap, loosening a cascade of silver-white hair. She smiled and Pippa felt her knees almost buckle and the cheeks of her arse clench.

While Ella was clearing away Pippa set a long match to the already laid log fire in the hearth, lit several large church candles and dimmed the lights. She brought the wine bottle and two crystal glasses with her from the kitchen into the sitting room and set them on the oval Georgian coffee table

It's not as though she doesn't know after all, its public knowledge that I'm that way inclined and as far as I know this company is run by gays and she might change her mind, In the flickering amber warmth of the firelight, the candles created dancing shadows on the walls and Pippa, settled herself comfortably on the shabby chic leather Chesterfield sofa. She sipped the chilled wine, slowly stroking the dark brown luxurious fur throw, indulging herself in the notion of rivulets of hot steamy water flowing over that deliciously tanned body. Good God! Stop it woman, you don't even know her bloody name. Then again, the best thing for a hangover is a hair of the dog that bit you. Isn't it? She considered.

When Ella came back downstairs, she looked at the two glasses, the candlelight glistening in the crystal, and the flickering tongues of orange and blue of the fire crackling in the warm glow and she knew instinctively that Pippa didn't want to be alone. She smiled to herself and accepted the offered wine, "Just one, okay. I'm Ella Michaels by the way."

"Ah! You're the boss I believe, no wonder it looks such a good job."

"I suppose I am in a way but don't tell my partners." Ella laughed.

Of course, it hadn't stopped at one. They had talked long into the early hours, about everything, Pippa's tennis career, her love life, Ella's lack of one and a good deal about Ella's sculptural work. They had laughed long and hard at Pippa's presumption that Ella had been one of the gay partners of the company and when Ella had taken a joint from her antique gold cigarette case, saying, "Do you mind, I don't do it very often, just occasionally when I really want to relax." They had settled to an easy rapport.

Ella had been so gentle, had stroked Pippa's neck, caressed her throat, her touch like no other Pippa had ever experienced, as soft as gossamer wings, light as a summer breeze across her skin, sending shivers of pleasure down her spine.

"You have a wonderful touch, great hands."

"Why thank you, madam," Ella laughed, "I suppose it's kneading all that clay that does it."

They had kissed, sensual, warm, their lips barely touching, Pippa had tasted Ella's hot sweet breath, and they had gone to bed giggling like schoolgirls and curled up together. Whilst Ella lay, her sleep distorted silver tresses fanned out on the dark black silk pillow Pippa had rolled onto her side, propped her head up on one arm and watched her, listening to her soft rhythmic breathing, longing to touch her, to let her lips trail across her breasts, so tempting, she touched herself lightly, then slowed her racing breath and allowed her desire to subside.

Chapter Seven

Ella was sat on one of the comfortable rose velvet sofas in the majestically high double-story lounge of the hotel its ceiling covered in hand-wrought warm peach moldings and covings, the Georgian paneled walls trimmed with white architrave. She was admiring the large French-style ormolu clock mounted above the Adam fireplace. The clock didn't appear to be working and Ella chuckled to herself imagining that Joy would simply say it was at least right twice a day. An old chestnut of course, but Joy's deadpan delivery would still make them laugh. The room with its' massive Doric sienna marble columns, heavy dark oil paintings, and plush green carpeting had a seductive elegance. Antique console tables with elaborate flower arrangements on them and small coffee tables were strategically placed around the room and a grand piano stood to the right of the fireplace. Ella wondered if it was ever played. A grand piano had been her mother's greatest desire; they had always had an upright one and in one of the few times they could stand one another's company the family had sung together Elizabeth accompanying she played well but only by ear.

The Grand was probably the finest hotel in Eastbourne and Ella was not surprised to find that the top tennis players and commentators were also staying there. She stood and greeted Pippa when she arrived for their pre-dinner drinks and they talked through the coming exhibition.

The show, entitled 'PRISONERS' contained six major bronze sculptures, all on the one theme and some six other pieces using a range of mediums and varying in sizes. Pippa had brought along the catalog, which was being distributed to major buyers and art collectors throughout the world inviting them to the open night and the subsequent auction following the close of the show one month later. The catalog described the Tate's excitement at discovering what it referred to as 'The New Mistress of The New Millennium', the finest sculptor to emerge since the age of the Old Masters, their greatest coup for this the year 2000.

"You really are getting nervous about this? Cold feet, or should I say cold hands? Pippa enquired with concern reaching out and touching Ella's hand. Ella almost flinched. Since the one night they had spent together Ella had avoided any intimate contact with Pippa.

"I'm sorry, I'm sorry Pippa, yes, it's just nerves, what if people don't agree with all this hype, and then I'll be as naked as the day that I was born?" She gently squeezed Pippa's hand in apology.

"I don't really get that___ and anyway it's not hype, you are the finest sculptor of this age, it's time you realized it."

I have no formal training as you know, just twelve months on a fine arts foundation course. I gave it up I was convinced that I wasn't any good at art."

"No good? How could you have thought that?"

"I was surrounded by other students who when looking at a painting of a small yellow square in the top right hand corner of a white canvas with four black lines traversing it two horizontal and two vertical would go into paroxysms of delight at the brush strokes and discoursed forever on how long it must have taken the artist to decide on the position of the black lines. I couldn't see what they saw and neither could I paint it, I tried but I was only lying to myself so I gave up and went into design. I had a grant, which for people like me was a necessity no family money, and I worked as a croupier in a casino most nights."

The story of the Emperors' New Clothes is an analogy for what good public relations and tame critics can do for half a dozen house bricks laid on the floor. If you convince enough people that it is art they will believe it because people generally don't want to appear unknowledgeable or lacking in taste.

"Anyway, I hope you're right and the critics don't become the one small voice in the crowd. Criminals are entitled to a trial by their peers but unfortunately not artists, critics, who would give anything to have the real gift but don't, often take out their frustration on those who do. As they say, those who can DO those who can't TEACH and the rest criticize."

Pippa shook her head and laughed at Ella's fears. "Mihailovna wants me to introduce you to her. What did you do to her? She's not normally quite so persistent."

Ella smiled and shook her head, "Nothing, really I didn't do anything. It was her that did something to me, she practically stripped me with her eyes, I felt weird, honestly. Does she do that to everyone she takes a passing fancy to?"

"No, I've never really known her to make a play for one of the spectators before. I wouldn't pay much mind to it if I were you, she can be nice when you get to know her but predatory and notoriously promiscuous."

"Have you fucked her?"

"For God's sake Ella, you like to shock people every now and again don't you?"

"Not for God's sake, for mine, I'm just asking, just curious."

"Well for the record, yes we had a brief fling some years back. She's very good, very sexy, very sensual, but there was no love in it between us, more a conquest for her, she's very controlling I think in some ways it feeds her aggression on the court and we never carried it on after the tournament was over. She's become very Americanized since she became a nationalized citizen and anyway I'm hardly in her class as far as tennis is concerned. I'd go so far as to say she's the greatest tennis player ever and with nine wins at Wimbledon to her credit, I doubt she'll ever be matched. Still, I think her reign is over now, too many up and coming young players. She'll probably retire after this year that is unless she manages to win another title and then who knows?"

"Is that likely? Personally, I've always admired her for her play; I'd like to see her go out in a blaze of glory."

"Gaffy is a sexual predator I already told you; she's extremely manipulative you watch out. What she says she wants is for you to do a sculpture of her but I doubt that's all she's after. However I did promise to ask you, so what do you think?"

Ella pondered the question, "Could be a good piece. She has such tremendous power; she strikes me as very self-possessed unafraid of who she is. I admire her. You could bring her to Lincolnshire, I could do the preliminary measurements and sketches and the like in the studio. It would probably take two sessions, perhaps you could persuade her to stay over for a weekend. I could invite Joy and Ao they'd love that and yourself of course."

Ella secretly hoped that Pippa would pass this time she was intrigued by the idea of getting to know Mihailovna better.

Chapter Eight

The helicopter hovered above a large Georgian house set amid its own grounds, nestling in the spectacular greenery of the Lincolnshire Wolds.

"Is this it? It looks quite grand." Mihailovna smiled to herself in anticipation. Her conversation with Pippa had turned out better than she could have imagined, not only was the woman beautiful but she was also wealthy in her own right and judging by reports, talented too. Mihailovna often worried when encountering new people, especially if she desired them. She had made the occasional foray acting on her instincts only to find much to her chagrin the object of her desire was more interested in basking in her glory rather than her arms.

Joy came out to meet the arrivals, greeting Pippa with a light peck on the cheek and offering her hand to Mihailovna, taking in her athletic stance, the way the pale green silk shirt and baggy green trousers reflected the color of her eyes.

"Hi! I'm Joy."

I'm sure you are thought Mihailovna smiling to herself.

"I'm one of Elly's business partners, though I don't have much to do with it these days as I'm usually busy, but I wouldn't have missed the opportunity to meet you for the world. I've been a fan for years."

"I've seen you before, in the Garden Club in London, you're the singer comedienne. I loved your act; you were really funny especially the takes on Edina and Patsy from Ab Fab, good singer too blues and jazz but I also enjoyed your interpretation of Leonard Cohen."

"Well, thanks. That's right I do spot there occasionally. So you like 'slash your wrists now' Leonard Cohen, also one of Elly's favorites strangely enough." Joy's handshake was warm and firm.

"Elly has asked me to show you to your rooms and around the house, she's busy working in the studio right now but when you've settled your bods we'll join her there."

Joy chattered and joked all the way to their respective rooms.

"This is your's Pippa, but then you know your way around here, more or less, so I'll leave you to it; see you downstairs in the sitting room when you're ready. This is your's….I'm sorry I don't know what to call you I've only ever heard you referred to as Miss Mihailovna and if I say that I'll sound like a tennis referee, won't I?"

"Most friends call me Gaffy, and it's a tennis umpire," she laughingly corrected.

The bedroom was large and airy. Mihailovna looked around her admiringly. The old oak floorboards had been whitened and distressed and the walls were ivory white with painted wisteria cascading from the old wooden picture rails. There was a four-poster bed draped with white muslin, billowing slightly in the light breeze, pale, lilac and white, linen dressed the bed. The furnishings were French antiques, painted white and distressed with the occasional touch of gold: the wisteria motif was repeated sporadically on the larger pieces. The room had a Mediterranean charm, its aged elegance airy and flooded with shafts of sunlight.

Joy opened the French windows wider and walked out onto a broad balustrade balcony running the full length of the rear façade of the house. She and Mihailovna stood looking down onto a magnificent mosaic-tiled swimming pool. Six enormous stone pillars bought from a reclamation yard, three on either side, flanked the pool supporting the empty sky and a carved stone bench from the same job lot sat at the head giving the pool a Romanesque appearance. Bronze life-size sculptures, two of them, small children, sitting giggling and thrashing their feet in the blue water, and the other a nubile young girl, her breasts just budding, was dipping the toes of one foot tantalizingly into the pool.

"Superb aren't they? There's actually a motor moving the children's feet, she's so inventive is our Elly. I love her to pieces."

They moved back through the bedroom and into the corridor.

"That's Elly's room there," Joy threw at Gaffy, waving her hand in the direction of the next door on the landing. She led them down the wide staircase and into the sitting room where Pippa and Ao waited. Joy pointed out an antique drum table that was covered in some black and white and some colored photos, of various sizes and all in different frames. She lifted one of a handsome young man and a beautiful young woman.

"Elly's children, good looking kids but they are really nice, very well brought up." She placed the ornate silver-framed photo back on the table.

After further introductions whereby Gaffy's fear that Joy was Ella's partner was allayed, they proceeded to inspect the other rooms and introduce Gaffy's chef who traveled everywhere with her to Joseph, Ella's Chinese cook who was busy preparing lunch.

"Shall we find Ella now?" Pippa interceded, impatiently.

Chapter Nine

Ella was in her studio which had been the old coach house, wearing her usual work clothes, the scruffy black vest and shorts, a worn baseball cap at a jaunty angle, working on a figure of a nude female. The form was reclining backward, its weight resting on two unformed stump -like arms the whole supported by metal armatures. Ella's hands were massaging the wet clay, sliding slickly down the right stump, giving it shape and life, her hands moved back across the shoulders creating a graceful curve to the outstretched neck.

"Elly, this is Gaffy, Gaffy, Ella Micheals."

Their eyes met and held for a moment.

"We've met, kind of," smiled Gaffy and raised her eyebrows questioningly.

"Kind of," Ella responded, "but I won't offer to shake hands right now." She indicated her wet, slimy, clay caked hands.

Pippa frowned, looked from one to the other, and moved away; resenting the feeling that somehow something was happening that she wasn't a part of.

"Joy, would you do the honors, please? I'm not being ill-mannered, I'm listening, but I probably won't look up very often I just want to finish off here."

Gaffy watched in silence, fascinated, mesmerized by the movement of Ella's hands, it was, she thought so intrinsically sexual. It was very warm in the studio and small beads of perspiration slid down towards Ella's breasts, Gaffy gave an inaudible sigh, she thought it looked like Ella was melting.

"What is this?" asked Gaffy indicating the piece Ella was working on. "I mean I can see it's a woman but is it commissioned or anything?"

"This, well if you look behind me, there are some photos of three young women, naked in the rain, I had to pay them quite a bit to do that, then there should be some sketches of them in particular poses, the other two figures, one of them is being cast and the other here she indicated a tall structure swathed in a wet sheet, is almost finished, it's at the leather stage, but it still needs some final work before casting, and this one, this one I'm working on. When they're all molded, they'll be poured in wax, I'll make any final adjustments, and then they're cast in bronze. Sorry, too much technical jargon___"

"No, please, I'm interested."

"They're going on the front lawn. I've always had an inkling to dance naked in the rain; it seems the quintessential act of liberation and abandonment."

"Do you hanker to be liberated?"

Ella chuckled at the thought, "Yes probably, sometimes I think I'm a bit too anal, though I do have my moments.

"They're not for sale?" Gaffy questioned.

"Do you play tennis because you want to or because it's made you rich and should I say infamous?"

"Because I want to, but I accept the trophies."

"Every sculpture I make, I make for my own pleasure, and creation is its own reward. Occasionally a someone has come along who wants the piece for themselves for the sheer pleasure it will give them each time they look at it, touch it, and caress it, but I can't bear to part with them. I could offer them a second cast that has been slightly altered from the original___ at least I have considered doing that, but selling the pieces is part of the deal in the exhibition coming up, so I suppose I have to live with that."

"What if I offered to buy them?"

"Then we might discuss it, but this isn't the time."

She stopped working as Joy rejoined them, bringing a bottle of chilled Perrier Jouet, Cuvee Belle Époque, the flower etched bottle was one of a very rare batch decorated with a design by Makoto Azuma who had been invited to expand on Emile Galles original design for the millennium year, and two large beautiful Baccarat crystal champagne flutes. She offered one to each of them. Ella rinsed her hands, dried them and then applied moisturizer from a wall dispenser, the moisturizer had a light herbal fragrance that teased at the senses. She removed the baseball cap and allowed her hair to tumble across her shoulders, lifted the glass to her lips and looking over the rim into Mihailovna's eyes, drank deeply.

The further, south-facing end of the studio was an enormous glass conservatory, Japanese lacquered furniture was arranged amid a riot of exotic plants and flowers, and the humid atmosphere was made bearable by two huge ceiling fans, which thrummed as they spun, moving the air as a summer breeze the scent of the exotic plants was heady. Gaffy and Ella joined the other three there.

Shortly Ella stood to leave. She touched Gaffy's shoulder lightly, applying a little pressure and quietly excused herself whilst she showered and changed. Joy observed the small judder and shift of the shoulders Gaffy gave and exchanged a mischievous little smile with Ao.

Half an hour or so later Ella rejoined the others on the patio outside looking fresh and bright, dressed in an ecru short-sleeved, scooped low neckline top and matching wide-legged trousers in raw silk. Ella rarely wore bright colors; they spoke too loudly of passion but preferred muted shades which allowed her to blend into surroundings making her less noticeable or so she imagined.

Joseph had laid out lunch by the pool light wooden baskets of Dim Sum. They laughed and giggled at one another's dexterity or lack of it with the ivory chopsticks provided as utensils and the champagne had put all bar Pippa into a relaxed mood.

"You were your normal devious self weren't you Gaffy, when you omitted to tell me that you had met Ella before?

"I did say it wasn't really a meeting, we never spoke."

"Knowing you, you didn't have to; I imagine you said all you needed with your customary leer."

Ella looked down at her glass to hide a sheepish grin and Joy interrupted in an attempt to diffuse any tenseness.

"So Gaffy, what do you think of Elly's taste in décor."

"I think it's very beautiful…that is, what I've seen of it."

"But you have seen it, come on now, what else do you want to see?"

"Well, you refused to show me Ella's bedroom." The remark was pointedly made to goad Pippa but Joy tried once more to lighten the mood.

"Oh! You don't want to be going in there, that's where Elly invites people to come and look at her etchings, and all of them are really lewd nudes, baby, men with all their dangly bits, ugh! Not for the likes of us, eh! Gaffy."

"Really Ella?" Asked Mihailovna disbelievingly.

"Well yes, but not quite as Joy puts it, there are nudes in there though."

"I swear to you Gaffy, there isn't a person in there with any clothes on."

Even Pippa managed to smile some throughout the rest of the lunch, feeling that Gaffy had been put in her place with regard to Ella's sexual preference.

On their way back through the house, Ella glanced at the drum table with the photos and quietly placed the photo of Crystal and Jasper in its original position.

Chapter Ten

Whilst the others prepared to swim or laze around for the rest of the afternoon Ella suggested to Mihailovna that they retire to the studio to get started on the preliminary photos and sketches.

Gaffy's thick light brown hair, golden flecked, bleached by the sun was cropped close framing her tanned weathered face. A Slavic face, high chiseled cheekbones, a firm chin cleft with a deep dimple and luminous peridot heavy-lidded eyes, deep set their corners etched with fine lines that deepened still further when she smiled. Her lips were full and well-shaped her mouth a little too wide for classical beauty, her nose longish and straight, the whole more exquisite than the parts. The lips especially seemed made to be crushed in a passionate kiss thought Ella Michaels as she scrutinized her subject.

"Do you have anything in particular in mind?" Asked Ella as she turned on the high wattage lighting and prepared the camera.

"I have a lot in mind actually."

"Yeah! Okay. I got the message. Now, you want me to do your bust, right?"

"Oh! Do I?"

Ella played with her lower lip; a small frown of concentration knotted her brow.

"Do you want this to be a portrait of you, the tennis star, or you, the person, or both? I mean, do you sleep with the racquet, are you intrinsically joined at the hip?"

"I sleep with women my love, as you and the rest of the world are well aware."

"Okay. Do you feel comfortable removing the shirt and posing as I ask?"

Gaffy merely removed the shirt revealing creamy patches of skin contrasting with the deep tan where her tennis outfits had protected her from the sun, small pert breasts, the nipples standing proud and incongruous in her young man's figure. She felt a tingle creep down her spine. Shuddered. causing her to flex her shoulders but she couldn't read the expression on Ella's face since Ella was staring into the camera.

"Just hold that look for a moment. Fine, now can we do some of your more classic expressions, like punching the air, okay? That one where you pull your clenched fist downwards, like so? Good, now look at me as though I'm your opponent and you're about to serve. Fine, now relax, look at me as though I'm the most desirable woman you've ever come across." She lowered the camera, and a dazzling smile lit her face, revealing white even teeth.

"I think you know how true that is," Gaffy said lowering her eyes to Ella's breasts, her tongue sliding across her upper lip.

"Hold that, please. Fine, thank you, that wasn't so difficult now was it?" Ella spoke as though Gaffy was a reluctant child who had to be coaxed to take their medicine. "You can put your shirt back on now," she said laughingly as she turned down the lights and put away the camera.

"I might like to leave it off."

"Fine by me. Now would you like to sit down whilst I take some measurements."

Gaffy laughed throatily, "You're really going to measure me?"

"Yes, but only your head, the length of your nose, the distance between your eyes, which incidentally is suspiciously narrow enough for me to believe you untrustworthy."

Ella approached with a pair of metal pincers. "This won't hurt one little bit I promise you, though I do have to get really close," and with that, she straddled Gaffy's lap.

Gaffy was conscious of Ella's slow even breathing in comparison to her own short rapid gasps, the dizzying scent of her filled Gaffy's nostrils, the heat of her body emanated from Ella in waves engulfing Gaffy's senses. She felt she wanted to plunge into and drown in the woman. She was unavoidably staring into the deep shadowed cleft of Ella's cleavage, felt a surge of desire rush through her and was conscious of her own wetness as Ella tensed her thighs, stared directly into the potent green fires of Gaffy's eyes, licked her lips, then dismounting and moving quickly aside she quipped, "Payback time. I think I owed you that."

Gaffy looked at her open mouthed, shook herself to dispel the longing and said, "You bitch."

Ella only smiled unconcernedly as she set about readying some artist's pencils and a pad.

"Fine, now we just sit still and quiet please and I do some sketches.

A much-subdued Gaffy still managed to throwback, "vengeance will be very sweet at the tasting."

"What makes you think I'll invite you to dine?"

Chapter Eleven

On the stone patio by the pool the group had eaten an 'al fresco' dinner, Lobster Thermidor, Moule Marnier and a host of other seafood delicacies prepared by Joseph and Mihailovna's chef, and had now retired with coffee and liqueurs to a seating area furnished with seagrass sofas and armchairs, sporting batik printed overstuffed cushions. Joy was strumming her guitar, singing, running through her repertoire of celebrity imitations, and telling jokes. The conversation was easy and the mood was light. Mihailovna watched Ella closely and occasionally their eyes would meet and they would exchange a small smile. As the evening turned chill, Ella shivered slightly and Gaffy immediately rose and placed her own cashmere shawl around Ella's shoulders her hands lingered for a moment on the nape of Ella's neck, their faces so close they could feel one another's breath. Gaffy was tempted to steal a kiss, but Ella shivered again gave a sharp intake of breath and stepped back, this time it was not caused by the chill of the evening.

Mihailovna woke early, showered, and went downstairs where she met Pippa and Joy.

"Breakfast by the pool Gaffy. We're going to use the gym first though and then a swim, join us if you like," Joy said brightly as Pippa went out the door.

"Where's Ella?" asked Mihailovna.

"Elly, she's already out, riding, probably in the ménage at her daughter's stables down the road a mile. Elly's an early bird, doesn't sleep well, sometimes works all night. Plus she likes her own space, when we stay over here she leaves us to ourselves, she'll join us when she feels like company."

"How come she's so distant?"

"You really fancy her, don't you? I've known her for years before I met Ao when she was married to John, and she's very difficult to get to know. Takes her a long time to trust anyone. Most people think she's just very laid-back but it's more than that, she does distance herself it's something to do with her childhood. She has five sisters and a brother you know but she never sees them. I think she paid them off years ago on the agreement that they never contact her again. Occasionally, when we've shared a joint she has opened up, that's how I know, but I never pry."

"Are you in love with her too? Pippa obviously is."

"I was. Maybe I still am a little, but with Elly, you have to learn to love from a distance. You don't strike me as the kind of person who would put up with that for too long, but if you just want a sexual encounter, well, who knows she's been celibate for some time now."

"I'm intrigued, let's just say that. Where do I find this ménage? I like to ride too back in the States I have a Western ranch, lots of horses, you should come sometime I'd love to see you rope a steer."

"That'd be the day," and Joy bubbled with laughter.

Mihailovna stood in the shadows beside the dressage ring, the only sounds, the slight creak of good leather, and the shuffling sough of hooves through the soft bark surface covering the ring. Ella was riding a magnificent Andalusian stallion, jet black, well-muscled, his thick neck arched proudly, the ringlets of his mane falling almost to his knees. His nostrils flared bright pink and he blew out steam as he changed leg repeatedly performing an equine ballet. Ella sat firmly, hardly seeming to move, the nuances of the signals she gave him went unnoticed they were so slight, yet perfectly attuned to his balance, his every movement. Completely focused, their dance appeared courtly, effortless, as they pirouetted in the shafts of sunlight, piercing the dim interior where dust motes stirred by his hooves executed their own dance macabre.

Mihailovna nodded to herself, appreciating the privacy of this moment, and retreated without a sound.

Ella let her mind drift riding back through time into the realm of memories. She remembered hiding from her brother in the dusty attic, riding the old iron bedstead an old flock pillow for a saddle, the tracks of tears on her cheeks, the blood from fifty or more puncture wounds, inflicted by the steel bristles of a hairbrush, drying on her small thin arm, her breathing tempered as she fought to dismiss her anger and dispel the murderous thoughts of revenge her vivid imagination was capable of conjuring. Memories were never far beneath the surface, a black cauldron simmering away on an eternal flame.

Chapter Twelve

There had been a time when she was just around twelve years old when she had thought death preferable to the constant onslaught of her brother's browbeating and violence. The violence had diminished somewhat after the time when he had thrown the book she was reading onto the fire, baring his teeth in a snarl as he waited to see how she would react and laughing turned his back when she refused to. Ella had suddenly found herself with a poker in her hand and in one swift movement struck. The sound of iron hitting bone had made her smile in return. She had found the sight of the blood running over his fingers as he clutched his head and slumped to the carpet quite satisfying. Ella had warned him that she would lie in wait when he was drunk and stealthily kill him with a knife, or lay a trap on the staircase, tripping him and plummeting him down the stairs to end in a broken heap at the bottom.

There had been repercussions of course but the violence had stopped, he had never struck her again, in fact, according to their mother he had confessed that he was a little afraid of Ella, no one else, but Ella he believed, there had been a coldness about her, a calculating iciness when she had made the threats.

The constant taunting and tyranny with which he ruled their home had though continued unabated and at twelve years of age, Gabriella Mickiewicz had purposefully drawn a razor blade across both wrists and sat calmly as she watched the darkening pools of her own blood grow deeper and waited for the peace of death.

A short time of peace that was not death did ensue, psychiatric evaluations, and a stay in a children's home which for most children would have been considered a trial something to fear, for Ella was a haven. The psychiatrists though gleaned nothing from Ella, she did not betray her mother's fear that had allowed her brother's tyranny and after a short court case was returned to the family home with a three year probation sentence. Suicide it seems was against the law.

Chapter Thirteen

The probation officer assigned to Gabriella's case, Ruth Jacobs, handed Ella's file to her supervisor after three months marked, CASE CLOSED.

"This isn't like you, Ruth, giving up."

"Believe me Bill, this case is like no other. I think the kid needs a psychiatrist, not a probation officer, she is one weird cookie. The first day, she comes in sits down and says that the law is forcing her to come here, she has done nothing wrong, everyone deserves the right to their own choices and from now on she will never ever speak again and all this, would you believe, from a twelve-year-old. And I tell you that is it; she never has, in three months. I have tried everything, even tried to bribe her with some clothes of my daughter's that she doesn't wear anymore, good things, designer label stuff. That kid looked at me as though I was an alien or something she had stepped in and failed to wipe off her shoe. Just after that she brings a book with her every session, sits and reads for half an hour then gets up and walks out. Honestly, she makes me feel guilty, inept, useless."

"Twelve-year-olds don't try to top themselves for no reason, Ruth. You tried the family, school, why did she do it?"

"Bill the original hospital reports stated no sign of sexual abuse, a few old fractures could have been anything. The school reports state that she is above average intelligence, straight A's, popular with other kids, the only little glitch, none of them ever get invited home. Visited the mother, the house is clean, in fact overly so, mother's a bit OCD. The kid is not malnourished, is well dressed, as far as their budget goes, school sweaters tend to be hand-knitted not shop bought, that kind of thing. The mother said Gabriella felt that she had not committed any crime and saw no reason to be associated with other kids who had. I tell you, Bill, that kid is tightly wound, something going on there that I can't put my finger on. Whatever it is, nothing I do or say is going to change it, waste of time and effort."

"Sounds to me like she likes to be in control of herself, lots of suppressed urges, a time bomb primed to go off one day. I agree with you Ruth, waste of time for us, CASED CLOSED.

Also watching Ella, from the shadows, stood Adam Fergusson. Fergusson was a retired SAS Major, who lived alone in the old gatehouse to what was the original estate. He was tall, six feet two and still in good shape for fifty, his complexion tanned, weathered by the elements and his salt and pepper gray hair, now allowed to grow to shoulder length, he wore drawn back in a ponytail.

A quiet, meditative, private man who spent most of his leisure time walking in the surrounding countryside, occasionally bringing home and tending injured animals. His reputation as something of a healer had spread throughout the villages and local children often brought their pets to him. Ella's daughter Crystal and he had become great friends and he often worked with her and Ella's horses. He had been helping Ella with the black stallion, Velvet, who had a tendency to shy when confronted by the smallest sound and Fergusson was fast developing a growing fondness and admiration for Ella. Now both he and Crystal joined Ella as she dismounted.

"Alright Mommy? You can leave him with us; we'll see to him, you should get back to your guests. One of them was here watching, Adam says"

"Oh! Which one, Mihailovna?"

"Aye, that would be the one. The Russian"

"You sound as though you don't like her," Ella observed as she watched Fergusson's strong capable hands moving across the horse's back, gentling him.

"I've no opinion, either way."

"He's much better, don't you think Adam?" asked Crystal.

"Aye, aye he is" Fergusson answered.

He's as economic with his speech as he is with his movement Ella thought as she watched Fergusson walk away leading the horse.

Chapter Fourteen

Fergusson and Crystal stood outside Velvet's box.

"You like my Mom, don't you?"

"Aye, I like her well enough."

"Come on Adam, I think you like her a bit more than well. How come I've never seen you out with any women?"

"When I was in the service, I didn't think it fair. Too much to ask of a woman, to be always waiting, not knowing if yer man was coming home or not. It was easier not to bother."

"And my Mom?"

"Yer Mother's a beautiful and talented woman. What's not to like?

"You might be safer to admire her from afar, she's not very good at relationships, ask my Dad. I don't think she ever trusted anyone enough to love them, apart from my brother and me."

"Aye, well, maybe that's something your mother and I have in common," sighed Adam, "we all have our demons."

Crystal wondered what Adam's were; she was aware of what some of her Mother's were. She knew some of the history, knew that she had aunts and an uncle that she rarely if ever saw. Her Mother was reticent, didn't like to discuss it but fragments drifted in here and there. Ella had deep scars on either wrist, and had said that there was a time when she hadn't wanted to live in this world, had wanted to slip into a world of her own making.

"She's worried about this exhibition. She's never put herself forward before for public criticism, her work's a very private thing for her."

"From what I've seen of her work, I haven't seen the Prisoners series but these here, and the one in your house in particular; I don't think she'll be having any trouble from the critics."

Crystal had been born in 1975 when Ella had been merely twenty years old but Ella had been enchanted with her since the first moment she had set eyes on her. Now twenty-five Crystal with her long thick dark tresses, almond shaped eyes and olive skin pertinent to her father's Jewish heritage and her conflicting sapphire blue eyes their irises darkly outlined identical to her mother's, and the lids fringed with long dark lashes, was now a mother in her own right.

Crystal had been a page three model, on the fringes of fame, had flirted with drugs and alcohol but meeting Matt had steadied her, they shared an enduring love of horses and had with a little help from Ella who owned the land set up the riding and livery stables close to Ella's home.

When Crystal and her husband, Matt, had had their first child, Ella had made them a sculpture of their hands entwined, holding their newborn child, in an embryonic pose, portrayed in bisque porcelain. It was a beautifully sensitive and highly emotive piece of work.

"Everyone who has ever seen that piece talks about it, all our friends love it. She presented it to us at the naming celebration we had for Xenon. We had no idea that she was even making it she must have used photos taken on the day we brought him home from the hospital."

"Is that what they're calling it these days," Ferguson laughed quietly, "when I was young we called it a Christening."

Jane Dee Simpson "Prisoners of our own device"

"I'm sure they still do Adam if you're a Christian."

Chapter Fifteen

Ella joined the others later for a swim and asked Gaffy if she could do more preliminary sketches.

"I watched you riding earlier, you're very controlled, where did you learn?"

"Oh! Well, my mother used to play the piano, totally by ear, you understand, and when I was a child, she had this great idea that if I took piano lessons I could fulfill her dreams and become a famous pianist, but I had other ideas at the time, though I often look at pianos with a kind of longing these days. I would love to just sit down and play one of my favorite pieces. She used to give me five shillings to pay for the lessons and I used to go to a local riding stable and take riding lessons instead." Ella laughed.

"Didn't she find out?"

"No, not really, here in England we used to have what we called the eleven plus exams. Children took an exam to determine which kind of school they went to, I passed to go to the grammar school and my elder sister bought me a bike, a horrid pink thing, called a Pink Witch, I'd wanted a pony. I sold the bike to a rich girl at school, told Mom I'd had it stolen from outside the fish and chip shop, went, and bought a pony from a local farmer. Every morning I went out early to the stables, with my school uniform in a bag, and I cleaned out and fed around ten horses, then back again when school was over, to bed them down. My family never knew they'd have said I had grandiose ideas. I had private lessons and my ponies keep. Lord, I must have stank when I was in class." They both giggled at the idea. "I was rather a 'tomboy' actually, I hated girly things, in fact, I thought girls were silly. They used to want to go and push somebody's baby about in a pram. I hated the idea, couldn't see any point. I don't think I thought about having children, the first one I ever held was Crystal."

"I never had any real childhood, not in the normal sense. In Russia, there were was either the very poor or those with special privileges because they were considered protégés. I earned my families' privileges by playing tennis and playing tennis and playing tennis. I defected on the advice of my coach but on reflection I needn't have, perestroika was on the way, glasnost, and communism was on the out," Gaffy said, "but then again, I love the game and look where it got me. Tell me more about you___"

It appeared to Gaffy as though a shadow passed over Ella's face, and slammed a door in Gaffy's, as Ella put aside the drawings and announced, "I have enough here to work with. If you'll excuse me I'll get on with this sculpture."

Gaffy hadn't been dismissed in such a way for a long time, and totally miffed she walked out of the studio and flounced up to her bedroom to be alone.

That evening Ella explained that she would work steadily on the bust of Mihailovna over the next two weeks but that she needed complete solitude, however, Mihailovna did secure a promise from her that she would take her up on her offer and sit in the players' enclosure during the whole of Wimbledon as Gaffy's guest.

Chapter Sixteen

"You've seen the brochures? The color illustrations don't do justice to the works Ella, the real emotive power of the 'Prisoners' can only be felt when you are in their presence. The sculptures will be at the gallery in two days, you'll be there won't you? To help set up the exhibits."

"I think they are over the top a bit the brochures as I said before, but yes, of course, I'll be there."

"No, I don't. There aren't enough superlatives to describe the pieces."

"But comparing me to the 'Old Masters', I still say that's a bit much."

"Not at all. They have already been sent out to most of the world's major art collectors and believe me, they are interested. You seem a little edgy, still nervous?"

"Yes, never done this before. You can convince yourself and hold the dream forever but once you put yourself out there you are inviting people to throw eggs at you and to destroy that dream and if that happens what are you left with?"

"That isn't going to happen, relax. How is the Mihailovna piece?"

"Good, I think, being cast as we speak."

"Do you hear from her?"

"Oh! All the time. She phones. I'm here for the Wimbledon fortnight also, going to be sitting with her coach, etc, I'm really looking forward to it___quite exciting."

"She has designs on you."

"I know." Ella shrugged, "She intrigues me. I really don't know where I'm going with this."

"But you are NOT gay."

"I don't subscribe to labels Pippa. I'm just a person and sometimes I'm lonely."

"What?"

"Yes, lonely. Loneliness is not always about the number of people in your company sometimes it's about the quality of the company you keep. I'm not lonely for sex per se, but for something, someone. I haven't done very well in the relationship stakes so far."

"You are too in control that's why I think men find it intimidating and you are distant sometimes."

"I don't mean to be, I've just been focused and whenever I've let someone get to me, my work has suffered, it's as though I don't have enough emotion to go round. I put it all into each piece. Gaffy and I are not in a relationship, at least not yet. I find the game adds some piquancy. A little thrill and I'm relaxing now that I've finished the work for the exhibition."

"You cannot play games with Mihailovna, she is a games master. I had hoped you were staying for the entire tournament but I was looking forward to us spending some time together."

"We will, I'll be at Wimbledon when I'm not at the gallery and I'll see you some evenings and when we are at the gallery, setting up.

Chapter Seventeen

Mihailovna trounced her early opponents during the tournament and Ella fell into an easy and enjoyable rapport with most of the players during their off-hours, she found them and their company a refreshing change to spending so much time alone with her own thoughts or with Pippa and her constant talk of the exhibition. Ella and Gaffy shared several evenings together with Gaffy's entourage; even dining at the Garden Club a highly exclusive and expensive dining club frequented by a good many high profile women some publicly lesbian and others who preferred to keep their sexual proclivity private. On this evening Joy was guesting.

"So Gaff, still got the hots for her eh?" questioned Joy, with a shake of the head and a knowing smile whilst Ella was out of hearing.

"She puzzles me, I really want to get to know her but sometimes it's like one step forward and two back."

"Yeah, yeah, get to know her eh! That in the Biblical sense?"

"Not just that I really do want to know her. Does nothing ever rattle her cage, dent the armor?"

"Oh! I've seen her rattled, you think she's all soft and compliant full of lofty thoughts and ideas but underneath she's made of sterner stuff than many may imagine, hates to be a victim and can be quite cold and steely when she sets her mind.

Once when we were first starting out in the decorating business, Elly and I had been working in an Indian Restaurant, marbling all the walls, working during the night for these people. The job was to be for cash, you know, avoid the VAT, anyway, job finished and they gave her a cheque. She wasn't too happy but asked John, her husband to go to the bank with it while we stayed there to clear up the paints and brushes, etc. John called her from the bank and told her the cheque bounced. She just walked calmly round this restaurant placing open tins of paint here and there around the walls. This Indian guy asks her (and here Joy develops the Indian accent) 'What you do?' She tells him, he has contracted her to paint his walls and she has not finished. If he doesn't find the cash in one hour she is going to repaint them. Throw the fucking paint everywhere. John got back, the Indian

pleads with him to stop her, saying 'She will not do this?' he seems
to think that because John is a guy like him, Elly will do what she is
told. John just laughed and said, 'Oh, believe me, she will'. Indians
0, cowboys 1, they paid, cash."

"Is that true?' Gaffy laughed.

"Oh yes, according to John it had happened once before with a
client of his, landscaping jobby, clients wouldn't cough up. Elly goes
there with a small digger and says she will re-landscape for them, she
has kids to feed. But that was John, no backbone, nice guy but Elly
lost respect for him. Elly admires strength, not the pumping iron type,
the strength of character, determination type. Sometimes I think she
wants to be dominated a little, she tends to go for older guys, father
figures that is when she goes for any." The conversation changed tack
as Ella returned.

"Not playing poker tonight, sweetie? Joy asked Ella.

"You play poker? Doesn't seem very English ladylike."

Ella laughed a low rakish sound and fixing Gaffy with a wry
smile she crossed her legs with a whisper of linen, "Oddly enough it
seems to free up my subconscious creativity. I can often solve a

problem with a piece of work after a few hours playing poker. We all have our vices."

Gaffy's insides lurched at the slight glimpse of thigh, as the warmth spread from her thighs and she wondered again what it was about this woman that held her so enthralled.

Joy returned to the small stage for another spot announcing first that the next song was dedicated to Ella from Gaffy, and launched herself into the erotic words of Leonard Cohen's 'Take This Longing From My Tongue'.

Ella had strong veiny hands with long tapering fingers, she was caressing the wine glass stem absent-mindedly, her fingers sliding up and down to the bowl, Gaffy watched,

"Will you ever?"

"Ever what?"

"Untie for me your hired blue gown; take this longing from my tongue?"

Ella's cheeks flushed with heat and she sought to look anywhere but into Gaffy's eyes sometimes she thought Gaffy could see into her head.

Chapter Eighteen

The commentators and spectators began to notice the new face among Mihailovna's entourage in the guest seats and speculation was rife, it seemed almost as though Gaffy was playing for the woman, her constant glances in the woman's direction appeared to seek approval and the woman's applause and smiles were accepted as an honour bestowed.

Pippa, as one of the commentators, kept her own counsel, protecting Ella she thought from any adverse publicity prior to the exhibition.

Ella was spending more and more time in Gaffy's company much to Pippa's chagrin.

The two were alone for a change in Gaffy's rented house; they and the rest of Gaffy's team had been watching reruns of the other players still in the tournament, especially Jana Djochevnic, the seventeen-year-old wunderkind in her debut Wimbledon, but they had all retired to bed leaving Gaffy and Ella alone.

"She's having a great tournament so far, what do you think Gaffy?"

"She's lovely, and she can play. I might like to get to know her if her God awful mother ever lets her out of her sight. Maybe even coach her if I retire."

A smile crossed Ella's face without reaching her eyes and she rose to leave.

"Well, let me know if you do. I won't keep you, I'll be getting back to the hotel, so I'll say goodnight."

Gaffy rose and touching Ella's arm asked her to stay.

"Are you jealous? You know I want you."

"I don't believe I possess that sentiment. But on reflection, you have a reputation to uphold, Djochevnic is probably more your style." Ella was surprisingly curt.

"Ella please, I was just teasing."

"Either way I just don't think it would work Gaffy. I'm, I'm intrigued, and I er____ I think I want you, but I could let you make love to me and maybe I can't respond."

"Kiss me."

Gaffy drew Ella gently towards her, her hand buried in Ella's thick silver hair, her breath warm and sweet as her lips brushed lightly across Ella's eyelashes, down to her mouth, her tongue lightly probing Ella's lips apart. The sensation of a woman's' soft skin both surprised and tantalized Ella.

She sighed, releasing a low moan which pierced Gaffy's insides and the kiss became harder, greedier as she pressed her body into Ella's forcing her back against the cold wall, bit her lightly on the neck a little harder than playfully, found Ella's breast and allowed her hand to slide softly across it feeling the nipple rise and harden as she pinched it between her thumb and forefinger. Ella's back stiffened and she shuddered as though galvanized by an electric shock. Gaffy's breath became short and rapid as she ground her pelvis into Ella's and Ella felt the warm wetness seep between her thighs as Gaffy slid the halter top from her shoulders her lips tracing a pathway of ecstasy to

Ella's breast. She cupped the yielding mound in her hand, caressing lightly with her tongue before her teeth seized the erect nipple. Ella found the sensation was almost unbearable and her hips thrust towards Gaffy an automatic reaction of her increasing desire her need for fulfillment which suddenly jolted her, her body tensed expectantly in anticipation then her mind became confused, the strangeness, halted her, brought her hand up to Gaffy's chest and she thrust her away breaking the spell being woven between them.

"No, stop, please stop. I___ I can't."

"Oh Christ, oh fuck." Gaffy fought to slow her breathing to quell the rising tide of desire coursing through her.

"I __I'd better go."

"You can't, you can't just walk out, what the hell is wrong? Tell me, explain to me, come on_____" Gaffy almost shouted in exasperation.

"I don't___I wouldn't know what to do, where to put my hands, okay it may sound stupid to you, but I've never___"

"What? Never touched another woman, you've touched Pippa."

"That was different, I didn't, I didn't_____"

"Desire her, but you want me, I know you do, I can feel your hunger."

"It would be like you shagging a dead body."

"Oh Ella, you are far from dead. What is so scary about it for you, you think you are straight, but your body is telling you differently, telling me different. You told me about dressing in boys clothes when you were young, pretending to be a boy. You're gay Ella, you just won't accept it. Let me make love to you; let me show you it's a myth Ella, the great phallic fallacy, one perpetrated by men that women need a penis to orgasm. How many women really orgasm just with penetration? Do you?"

"No I don't, but you're wrong it isn't just the sex that is our problem____what are we really doing? I can't afford to get involved with someone, you live in fucking America for example, I live in England."

"Oh Jeez! People commute Ella."

"Oh! Lovely, just what I need commuter sex, and with your drive, how would that work Gaffy? In the time we were apart you would have probably have shagged half the Davis Cup Team."

"So that's it, I'm promiscuous is that what you are saying?"

"Most of the gays I've ever met are, sex is their main priority, they're preoccupied with it and they do it without thinking of the consequences whether they're in a relationship or not. Where is the love, the respect?"

"I'm just the same as every gay you've ever met then? Yes, Ella, I want sex with you but it's more than that, I do respect you, I do want to be with you."

"All my relationships have been flawed, I don't need another failure, I don't want to close another door. For me gay relationships are flawed, something is missing let's face it they rarely go full term."

"We'll see. I always thought I would grow old with one person, one woman ___ as it turns out ___ but it hasn't worked out that way so far, but it is what I want. And children."

"Oh Gaffy, what about children? And there also there's a problem. I am a good bit older I already have grown children, been there bought the T-shirt and I certainly am too old to be running around after toddlers."

"You wouldn't have to I___"

"Wouldn't have to, oh, so you'd be the Mommy and I'd be the Daddy eh?" Ella gave a cynical smirk.

"Jesus you can be quite a bitch."

Look I'm sorry___I'm confused and ___ I'm going. No, let me go, let me think."

Mihailovna slumped down in the chair, her fingers kneading the point near the bridge of her nose, trying to dispel her growing frustration. I should have convinced her, enticed her, anything to take this longing away, she thought.

She rang Ella several times the next morning, she had had little sleep and desperately wanted to clear the air between them after the argument, she thought, and sighed.

Chapter Nineteen

"Well Pippa this game is certainly not going according to the book for Mihailovna, I've never seen her so rattled, she seems to be looking over at her coach or the players' enclosure quite often and the unforced errors are piling up."

"Yes Lisa, I'm sure Helena can't believe her luck to be one set up and leading 4 – 2 in the second against the great Mihailovna in the semifinal. Helena is playing her best game but Mihailovna just cannot seem to get it together. Several unforced errors and of course 3 double faults so far."

Gaffy Mihailovna sat with her face in the purple and green Wimbledon towel, willing herself to breathe deeply, concentrate, and force Ella Michaels from her thoughts. She turned to the umpire, said she thought she had pulled a muscle in that last fall she had taken and asked for her trainer, a few moments of brief respite.

The umpire informed the spectators of the slight delay and Gaffy's trainer ran to her, sprayed something on her calf and started to massage the area. In hushed tones they murmured.

"Come on Gaffy, this is not you, get it together."

"I can't seem to concentrate, why didn't she come?"

"She rang; she can't get here, some problem or other." The trainer lied.

"Really?"

The umpire leaned downwards with a warning glance, the trainer left the court and Mihailovna stood shaking her leg, then jumping on the spot a couple of times to give credence to the fictitious injury.

In the player's box on court number one Jana Djochevnic's mother sat listening to events on centre court from commentary piped through an earpiece, Mihailovna's game is falling apart, she seems to be injured and my darling Jana is one set up and 5-2 in the second set she thought smiling to herself and giving a slight nod in the direction of her daughter, their secret signal that things were going badly for Mihailovna.

Djochevnic's coach turned to Jana's mother, "How goes it?"

Renata Djochevnic smiled again, "Mihailovna is in trouble, and with any luck we will have a final between my darling and Helena Korda. My Jana has worked so hard for this, she will be the youngest ladies champion ever and then there will be no stopping her it is what she has always wanted."

"It is what you have always wanted my dear," her coach muttered in an aside then louder.

"Why if you had never injured your wrist all those years ago, this could be you. His obsequiousness was obvious only to himself.

Renata flashed her large white teeth again in a simpering smile. The coach was highly paid and knew just how to butter up Jana's mother. The truth was that the mother never let up, Jana had no personal life whatsoever, fulfilling her mother's dreams was all the life she was allowed. Renata Djochevnic was an ambitious woman whose career had been cut short when she had broken her wrist in a riding accident. The fracture was light but allowed Renata to beguile herself with an excuse for her mediocrity as a tennis player and press the full weight of her aspirations on to her daughter. Her long suffering husband had finally left her, he had in effect he realized been merely the sperm donor. Renata had never shown any further interest in sex once the child had been born.

Back on centre court Mihailovna was putting up an incredible fight, Helena Korda had allowed a little complacency to creep into her game and was caught unawares by the turnaround and the renewed vigor with which Gaffy was running down every ball.

"Mihailovna had taken a couple of tumbles Pippa perhaps she was more hurt by them than at first thought certainly the visit from the trainer seems to have relaxed her tension."

"Yes Lisa, um that does seem to be the case, for sure Mihailovna seems under less pressure, moving better around the court and more importantly finally getting her first serves in."

"There has been some speculation Pippa about the absence of the missing mystery lady today, could that have accounted for some of Mihailovna's preoccupation?"

"Well Lisa, I___I'm unable to comment on that, but I doubt that a professional like Mihailovna would be too worried by someone's absence especially at such an important point in the tournament."

"Game, set and match Miss Mihailovna, Miss Mihailovna wins 2-6, 7-6, 6-2."

Chapter Twenty One

As Mihailovna left the court she was met by her coach and trainer and ignoring their congratulations and sighs of relief demanded, "What did she say Ella?"

"Nothing, she didn't call, bitch, not a word, I lied, had to, had to get you through this match."

"She didn't call?"

"No, as I said I lied."

Gaffy felt hollow inside, nauseous, dizziness overcame her and she had to reach out to steady herself. She walked back to the changing rooms like an automaton, in utter silence, not a sound penetrated her reeling senses. Her sense of self-preservation had by the time she had entered the dressing area turned her disappointment to an all-consuming anger directed at Ella.

Jana Djochevnic was waiting there for her a sycophantic smile plastered all over her lovely young face. Mihailovna took in her long shapely tanned legs, the golden expanse of bare flesh around her midriff, her wonderfully graceful neck leading down to the shadow between her budding breasts and with a crooked smile playing about her lips listened attentively.

"I waited to congratulate you, Mother cannot come in here. I am so awed at the idea of playing you in the final, I just cannot believe it. I have admired you so much all my life. It is just wonderful; you are such a great player, totally my idol."

Mihailovna allowed the flattery to flow over her like a soothing balm, to wash away the hurt. She smiled lasciviously thinking this is going to be so easy as she put her arm around Jana's creamy shoulders and leaned in towards her.

"You know this is going to be my final Wimbledon, well, more actually I am planning to retire. I'm really looking forward to our match on Saturday. Your coach___ "

"Oh, Mother's choice of course, she has known him for just years. Why? Would you consider coaching after you retire?"

"For someone with real potential I don't see why not, look why don't you join me for dinner, we could discuss it?"

"Oh I doubt Mother would allow that what with the big one coming up, but we could do some practice tomorrow together at Queens Club and maybe I could work on her."

"Yes, you do that, tomorrow then." She let her hand slide around Jana's temptingly bare waistline.

Chapter Twenty Two

The practice session went very well considering, there was no denying the girl had talent, a good serve, she moved with grace and speed and her backhand was tremendous, one day she would be a champion thought Mihailovna, but not on Saturday, not this time.

To take a young player and mould them into a world champion would be a good way to keep the game in her life and she began to warm to the idea of coaching Jana but even more to the idea of bedding her she told herself forcing Ella from her mind. She had tried to call Ella several times only to get the answering machine or to be told that Ella was busy with the exhibition. Gaffy invited Jana to tea later all very proper with her mother as chaperone of course.

Far from being horrified at the thought of Jana spending time with Mihailovna Renata having given the idea of her coaching her daughter some considerable thought had begun to actively encourage her daughter to take advantage of Gaffy's interest. There was no way that she herself could ever afford a coach as prestigious as Mihailovna. Renata had already ploughed every penny they owned into the child, given up so much of her own life to make this dream come true. If Mihailovna was interested in Jana, was well, really taken with her, what harm could it do.

Her simplistic view of life allowed her to project her own lack of sexuality onto her daughter, several great tennis players were lesbians after all she thought, it might even sway Mihailovna's game on Saturday and even if Jana lost what a coup the great Mihailovna taking Jana under her wing in the future would be. Renata little thought that it could be the wing of a vulture she was proposing her daughter shelter beneath.

"Ella, if you are there, please pick up. Please talk to me, I love you, I need to be with you." Gaffy tossed aside the mobile in anger. "I hate answering machines."

The answer machine blinked at Ella and she touched the button and listened hearing Gaffy's voice even was enough to make her catch her breath.

Chapter Twenty Three

Awakening, she tensed every muscle then slowly released them in a half yawn, threw aside the sheet and let the cool air from the open window wash her body. Her hands roamed her naked flesh, sliding deliciously across her breasts felt her nipples pucker and rise in response and reached into the core wetness of her being. She felt hot breath, soft female skin, a tongue flickering and shuddered as she orgasmed. She stirred spreading herself, reached out to the empty space beside her. A morning shade, making an infrequent visit but this time the phantom had a face, that of Agafina Mihailovna.

As the needles of steamy water dispelled the last mists of sleep Ella pondered on Gaffy's words, truth was, she had always needed oral sex to reach her climax. Was it a myth, a phallic fallacy perpetrated by men that left women feeling inadequate, forever searching, forever striving to achieve. Still the problem nagged at her, yes, she wanted Gaffy, but was it all one sided? She wanted to sink into the depth of those deep green orbs, to crush that wide mouth with her own but unfamiliarity stopped her there.

Gaffy's secretary Anna had never seen her employer and friend so down, they had made such a great couple she thought of Ella and Gaffy and she knew Gaffy was trying hard not the let the hurt of whatever had happened between them show too much. The decision made she lifted the receiver and dialed Ella's mobile.

"Hello Ella, please don't hang up this is Anna, I really am concerned about Gaffy, she is so cut up about whatever has happened. I don't want to interfere but you are so good together. She loves you, she really does. Please, please will you come to the final?"

"I'm sorry Anna, I really don't think its best if I come and today is an important day for me_____"

"Promise me you'll try to be there. I know Gaffy, I know that win or lose she is going to retire. She really intends to settle down, she wants a relationship, she needs it, please Ella try to be there for her. There's a party later tonight if you can't get to the final will you come, please, it would mean so much to Gaffy, I've never seen her quite this way with anyone before I know this is the real thing for her?"

"Tonight is the opening night of my exhibition and I imagine I'll be really busy, I have to be there. I'll try to get to the final I promise."

Ella was fraught with indecision, the morning's fantasy still fresh in her mind. She was afraid knowing that Gaffy had the power to hurt her afraid for her own survival.

Chapter Twenty Four

Jana shivered with excitement as she prepared herself in the changing rooms Mihailovna had scanned the box for any sign of Ella but finding none had wiped a stray tear from her eye disappointment etched across her face. She squared her shoulders and faced Jana Djochevnic.

"I'm so nervous____"

Mihailovna looked into her bright eyes filled with such devotion, smiled and leaning in to her touched Jana's expectant young face with a light caress, and drawing her mouth to her own softly kissed her lips. A sharp stab of desire pierced the younger woman. As the heat rose within her she pressed her mouth harder, the kiss more demanding. Jana had sought to unnerve Mihailovna a little in the hope that she might go easier on her during the game but Mihailovna had turned the tables on her, she had not counted on her own desire. This was much more sensuous and provocative than the fumbled petting she had so far indulged in whenever she found the chance to dodge her mother's constant vigilance.

Gaffy broke the contact, "Come now, play your heart out, try to forget where you are think of it as just another match like any other. Tonight you'll be my guest at the party whatever happens."

They walked through the corridors and across the main reception room housing the glorious trophies bearing the names of all the great tennis players of the past their path lined with officials and press photographers, their shoulders burdened with heavy sports bags holding several racquets, strung to perfection for their individual preference, spare T shirts, face wipes, energy snacks and drinks Agafina Mihailovna and Jana Djochevnic their nerves jangling with the sense of occasion.

Gaffy looked up to the vacant seat as she stripped the plastic wrapper from one of her racquets. This was all she had ever really wanted up to now, the fame, the glory, she thought back to her first coach, Ivan Kaminski, three times he had played the finals at Wimbledon but the trophy had always eluded him. She had been seventeen playing in the French Open 1987 when she had last seen him, he had cried then smiled as he watched her being ushered away by American agents and mouthed the words "Win it for me."

In the year 1990 she had held the famous silver plate above her head for the first time and had basked in her glory but now she knew this would be the last time, now she wanted something more, she wanted to bask in Ella's eyes, Ella's laughter. She had been sure that Ella was the one, how could she have been so wrong, had it really just been infatuation, the constant desire to win? She cinched the cotton band around her head tightly wanting to squeeze the voices with their interminable questions out and surreptitiously wiped a tear from her eye.

Jana Djochevnic was struggling to stop her legs tapping nervously, every fiber of her being was tingling, her hands shook as she held the Styrofoam cup to her lips. This was her one desire, the beginning of her journey; she skipped out onto the centre court, the theatre of her dreams.

Ella was listening to the commentary from outside the court, they said Mihailovna seemed distracted, was slicing her serves wide, losing the point to unforced errors, she dropped her opening service game and Jana raced to a 2-0 lead. Djochevnic was pulling the ball from the most unlikely of shots, her long legs speeding her across court, this was her big chance and the crowd was loving every moment, cheering madly as she took the set 6-4 in forty six minutes.

Gaffy's energy was draining away with her hopes, her body was lethargic, she was unable to run down the balls, trailing at 0-3 in the second set when Ella unable to keep away any longer slid into the seat alongside Anna. Gaffy caught the movement in her peripheral vision, fired a forehand shot straight at Djochevnic who instinctively dodged the ball leaving it a path to the far corner of the court. Mihailovna had three love games in a row, bringing them to 3-3 a pivotal moment in the mach. Some of the most inspired play ever seen at a ladies match at Wimbledon followed and Djochevnic could only shake her head, tossing the gleaming pony tail, as Mihailovna was infused with a new vitality her tough athleticism finally coming to the fore.

"Game and second set Miss Mihailovna, one set all, third set."

In the third set Djochevnic crumbled, her confidence sank like a stone as Mihailovna fired backhand top spinning balls their angle just too good, took advantage of every short ball with subtle drop volleys, sending Jana stumbling into the net, lobbing the ball high over Jana's head to drop just inside the line. Repeatedly Gaffy's backhand drove down the line and the occasional one Jana managed to reach and make contact with her impetus sent her out of court and she fell a victim to easy passes.

The final shot was a demoralizing brilliant drop shot just over the net. A resounding cheer rose up from the spectators as Mihailovna, dropped onto her knees, her head in her hands and wept. There was a standing ovation as she finally staggered to her feet but through the veil of her tears, she saw that Ella had gone. Gaffy had lost the wind beneath her wings but was gracious to Jana and the many fans that clamored for autographed balls, T-shirts and caps, threw her racquet into the crowd for one lucky youngster to catch and patiently sat through the interminable interviews by television crews and journalists with their constant barrage of questions but it was an empty victory, the light had gone out of her eyes.

Chapter Twenty Five

Shortly before leaving for the Tate Gallery Ella received a phone call from Crystal and Jasper wishing her well, this was not their scene and Ella felt that she didn't need them to witness the almost false face she may have to wear for the evening. The next call was from Joy.

"Hello, sweetie, all set for the big night?"

"Hello Joy, yes___still a bit nervous, but I'm getting there. I'm more concerned with this Gaffy business really."

"Well my love I saw the final and if you want my honest opinion I think she is crazy about you."

"But look at the problems___"

"You want her; she wants you, what's the problem?"

"The age difference for one, I'm fifteen years older than her, she wants kids, my kids are grown up I don't think I see myself running around after a toddler."

"Oh sweetie, look, in this day and age, she would bring up any children with the help of a nanny for God's sake. As to the age difference, what of it if you were a guy no one would think anything of it and anyway no one will."

"Oh Joy, I just don't know, I fantasize about her, she is in my head, in my dreams___ "

"Look sweetie; go for it, if it's just an infatuation it will fizzle out, if you never try it you'll never know. Go on go for it and break a leg tonight and ring me with the gory details tomorrow."

The reception was held in the Rex Whistler restaurant of the Tate Gallery, a sumptuous buffet with champagne had been laid out for the visitors and the mood was charged with sexual tension as is so often when the rich and powerful gather.

Ella had arrived fashionably late her hair was coiled in a French plait, loose strands framing her face. She had finally chosen the knee-length Versace black silk dress having discarded it once in favor of a pale blue silk shift cut on the bias she thought much less ostentatious than the black which she had bought in a moment of female madness for an astronomical price, when the image in the cheval mirror looking out at her had appeared washed out and drab she had returned to the little black number. After several changes and numerous moments of indecision, she decided against the adornment of any jewelry other than the one carat diamond stud earrings and the black velvet choker, with a solitaire two carat diamond whose brilliance shimmered and drew all eyes to the graceful curve of her neck and the deep shadow of her cleavage. Embarrassingly for her, there was a small smattering of applause as she entered and Pippa introduced her.

Pippa was elegantly at home amongst the lesser royalty, the occasional pop star, film star, the famous and the infamous and those whose only reason for being there was to bolster their fading images, she graciously received the accolades for having discovered this genius and brought her to the attention of the mega-rich consortiums and private buyers and collectors, Howard Tullman the Chicago buyer, Roman Ambrovich and Thyssen Carmen Cervera to name but a few, gathered for the feast.

Pippa approached Ella with two men in tow; she introduced one of them as Max Cauldwell and the other Peters his assistant.

Cauldwell was a large man, thick around the waist and hips which tapered downwards to two small feet, and upwards to narrow shoulders topped with a small almost pointed head. He had a tautly stretched pink complexion and sparse white-grey hair. His pale grey eyes were narrowly spaced apart and his small slash of a mouth a permanent grimace. He was wearing a mohair grey dinner suit with a slight sheen and a white dress shirt and as Ella watched him voraciously stuff whole canapés into his mouth, revealing small off white sharp teeth the only image she was capable of conjuring was of a great white shark, even his hand when offered and Ella politely accepted was cold and slick with perspiration and reminded her of wet fish. His assistant Peters who flitted around his master replenishing the ever disappearing food was his remora, the small cleaning fish who danced attendance to every shark and whose ministrations were grudgingly tolerated saving them from becoming the next meal.

When he spoke it was with the careful enunciation of a plumy parody of the upper-class Englishman and his sentences had the precise and clipped fashion of a man in a permanent hurry. Part of

Pippa's introduction had heralded him as the chairman and major stockholder of one the largest IT conglomerates in the world and the leading software developer of games and virtual worlds. He informed Ella that he was the highest bidder so far for the sculpture of a young girl bound and terrified, a kidnap victim of the sex slave trade.

She had been unable to stop herself from saying, "I think IT takes away people's imaginations especially when some youngsters seem to live only in these virtual worlds, you give them numerous addictive pursuits to become obsessed with, IT appears to steal peoples free will and where will the artists of the future come from I wonder when even their own lives are created for them and they have ceased to interact with the rest of society."

His cold eyes swept over Ella and his smile was more a snarl, she felt like his next meal, a chill caused her to shift her shoulders and raised goosebumps on her arms. She was grateful when his minion said, "Sir," and motioned to his wristwatch and he grunted a semblance of an apology as though it was strange coming from his mouth, and left abruptly. Ella could imagine him as the end buyer of some poor young girl, sold into the sex trade and was almost tempted to remove the sculpture from the sale when she was distracted by someone to her left speaking to her.

The speaker was a surprisingly tall handsome Japanese, he introduced himself as Hiro Takana, his perfectly cut features his thick black hair graying at the temples giving him a distinguished air, his low modulated voice, and genteel highly polished manner was the only favorable impression made on Ella that evening.

"Your creations Madam Michaels, can you bear to sell them? I imagine it might be like losing a child each sale a small death."

"But you are a collector Mr. Takana, are you not?"

"I confess I am though I sense a little disdain in you for that title. I no longer have the gift of creation. Do you have children Madam Michaels? Other than these." He gestured to the sculptures.

"I do, and they are very dear to me."

"I too had a child Kiko," for a moment his eyes clouded with sadness, "my one creation; sadly she was taken from me. She had leukemia. Death has no respect for riches and power; I could not buy her life for any amount."

"I am so sorry, I can think of nothing more painful than to bury your own child. Could you not have had more children?"

"Alas! That was not possible." He did not elaborate as to why. "Ah! Now my collections are my children." He gave a small resigned laugh.

Ella was stolen from his company by Pippa whisked along and further regaled with her constant asides of large bids already received and ticket revenue from expected multitudes of visitors clamoring to see the show.

Ella became increasingly disorientated, dissected by differing groups and shared out amongst them all. Many seemed bewildered that this sophisticated woman, and not some emaciated Bohemian look alike, should be capable of producing such work. She caught snippets of conversation and was stunned by the realization that the subject was herself. A spiraling rising tide of banality, where people scored points for how many artist's names they could drop into the culture pool with spouted learned epithets garnered from revues and overheard critics, the generally vitriolic Jerry Saltz and the more benign Australian Robert Hughes among them, and for their acquisitions each costing enough to feed the third world. Ella wandered, a forced smile pasted like a mask on her face as she was questioned as to her taste in art, what she thought of such and such a painter, or sculptor, some whose names she vaguely recognized but most of them unheard of before.

There was no one in particular here with whom she had any affinity, they did not need her here they had the sculptures and their triumph. Ella slipped quietly away. Secluded in her car she succumbed to a long-awaited cigarette laced with a little marijuana. It is over, it was a success, and no one is going to nail me to the proverbial cross I think, her mind told her. What she needed now was to relax, to laugh with a bottle of champagne, not a glass, to be with someone, yes to be with someone she cared about who cared about her.

She worried that the barriers she had developed to protect the most vulnerable part of herself had become so impenetrable her instinct for survival and her need for love had been warring for years, her caution like a wall, a prison that she had built around herself to keep her safe. The safety was an illusion though and the dangers of feeling too much no worse than feeling nothing. The walls were so dense that she could not reach herself anymore, could not plumb her own depths and couldn't find what she had been sheltering so carefully. Was it just the difference, Gaffy being a woman that excited her sexually? Ella was used to fantasizing occasionally to gain relief, but no, it was Gaffy herself that got her heart rate up, that made her blood rush and her pulse beat faster.

The phantom of the morning revisited her with its' yearning desire, Vive la difference, she thought and she drove off into the balmy night through the relatively quiet streets in the direction of Wimbledon Village.

Chapter Twenty Six

The tension of the Wimbledon fortnight finally over the ensuing party at Mihailovna's rented property on Canizaro Road in Wimbledon Village was in full swing. The buoyancy of the mood in which she had held high the silver Venus Rosewater Dish for the tenth successive time had dissipated when she thought of Ella's insouciance in not deigning to materialize to witness her triumph. Bitter thoughts of Ella posturing amid the lofty grandeur of her arty world the sycophantic Pippa following in her wake embedded themselves and she turned to find her own aficionado Jana, simpering, at her side.

On a subconscious level, Mihailovna was aware that the Ella Michaels she had fallen in love with was not that of her jealousy inflamed imagination but her massive ego was not capable of assimilating these facts at this moment. She took another large shot of Absolut and leaning in to young Jana breathed into her ear that Jana should go to Gaffy's bedroom and she would follow shortly.

Jana trembled with anticipation as she undressed and slipped beneath the sheets. Gaffy feigned a headache and her disappointment with Ella as her excuse to her friend and secretary Anna for wanting to be alone for a while undisturbed.

Half an hour later Anna's face lit in a beaming smile as Ella drifted into the room, she seemed a little breathless her eyes alight with expectancy were searching for Gaffy.

"Oh Ella, you came, Gaffy will be so pleased, she has been so upset about you."

"Where is she?"

"She couldn't bear it any longer darling, all this gaiety; she went up to her room to be alone. I'll go and get her for you."

"No, it's okay, I'll find her." And with that Ella rushed up the staircase towards the bedrooms.

Ella pushed the door of the bedroom open, "Gaffy I'm here I came_____" the words caught in her throat, strangling her at the sight of Mihailovna's naked body, her face contorted, thrusting at the raised twin pears of Jana Djochevnic's backside, who knelt as in prayer, a beatific smile on her face as she moaned her ecstasy.

"Oh my God, Ella." Gaffy thrust Jana away from her savagely and rose to face Ella.

Ella started to laugh hysterically at the absurdity confronting her, the black straps stark against the white skin, holding the engorged glistening wet fluorescent penis in place, the ludicrousness of what she herself had been contemplating.

Gaffy tore off the strap-on and reached out pulling Ella towards her, "It's not what you think, Ella, I_____"

Ella struggled against her, "Not what I think, no, no you're right, it's what I'm seeing, get away from me___, how fucking stupid of me to think, to believe I loved you, you have no scruples, no dignity." She pushed Gaffy back, felt the bile rising in her throat as she tried to free herself, her emotions corkscrewing out of control as a deep tide of anger and scorn at her own foolishness rose up from the depths and engulfed her.

"Please Ella, please listen." Gaffy's strong grip tightened on her dress clutching at the bodice, trying desperately to draw her back into the depths of the room. The dress tore exposing Ella's breasts.

"No, stop," Ella screamed, her fist connected with the fleshy part of Mihailovna's nose with a resounding thud and blood sprayed from her nostrils, she fell backward shocked by the unexpectedness of the blow.

How could she have loved this thing, this creature standing there, the molten lava of all past insults and aggressions overwhelmed Ella she screamed, her face distorted with fury, spittle flew from her lips as she launched herself at Mihailovna she wrapped her strong hands the knuckles white around Gaffy's throat and watched mesmerized as her eyes bulged and her face began to turn blue with the pressure.

Jana, knees drawn up tight to her head hunched her back against the headboard of the bed screaming, black tears of mascara tracked down her pale cheeks. Footsteps thundered up the stairs and into the room. Several hands wrenched Ella and Gaffy apart. Gaffy gasped for breath croaking, "Let her go, please, it's my fault."

Ella struggled free from the restraining arms holding her, fought her way through the throng of shocked white-faced people to the stairs and staggered down them her trembling hands trying to cover herself with the remnants of the black silk bodice. Mihailovna pulled on the grey sweatsuit that Anna, in a vain attempt to shield her nakedness from everyone, had pressed onto her and ran barefooted after Ella pushing aside anyone who attempted to stop her, catching up with Ella just as she reached her car leaned over and retched until her body emptied itself.

Ella turned, potent blue iciness shot contempt from her eyes wounding Gaffy to the core, her mouth full of intractable tension twisted in a snarl, and she shrank from Gaffy's bloodied face, from the evidence of her own violence, and stumbled backward into her car. The Supra's massive engine roared to life and shot forward, Gaffy trying to hang onto the door pleading with Ella to stop, was dragged painfully across the gravel for a few yards before being thrown aside bloody and grazed as the car shot through the open gates.

PART TWO

Chapter Twenty Seven

Two young constables sat eating their chips and fish, drinking cokes when the BMW 4W Drive, high wheelbase vehicle flashed past, careening from one side of the road to the other, sending the wheelie bin hurtling, crashing into the shops and spilling it's contents across the Wimbledon high street.

"Quick, bastards are obviously pissed, let's go."

Tossing the remainder of their supper into the back with the other chip papers and Styrofoam cartons they burned rubber as they lurched away. The siren wailed its' mournful cry as they joined the pursuit, increasing speed to match the fleeing vehicle. Adrenalin flowed as the excitement of the chase overcame logical good sense. As the cars flew through red lights, barely avoiding oncoming traffic the officers called on their radio for a stinger to be set up on major roads ahead, but the BMW veered off into the quieter, more salubrious avenues of Wimbledon Village.

The BMW driver glanced back through the haze of his drunken vision over his shoulder at the closing police car.

"Fuck me." He gasped as he turned back to peer ahead.

In that split second his vision registered an almost ghostly image, a white face, frozen in the rictus of a scream. The thunderous boom of a double impact and the tearing of steel rent the night's stillness.

Gaffy rushed headlong out of the gateway, shrieking for an ambulance, screaming Ella's name as she climbed frantically over the rear of the Toyota towards the body slumped the front seats, clawing her way to Ella, she drew back her head, cradling it to her chest. Blood glinted blackly, the flashing blue and red lights of the police car turning Ella's face into a kaleidoscopic horror mask, the blood was pouring from a gash in Ella's forehead and streamed from her nose and mouth.

"No please, oh God no, no, not now, not this." Gaffy pleaded, her head shaking, the tears streaming down her cheeks as she gently brushed the blood-soaked hair away from Ella's face.

There was movement, a low moan bubbled and rasped from Ella's throat.

The night was pregnant with a cacophony of car alarms and a symphony of undulating sirens, there was the hiss of escaping steam and the groans of tortured metal. A paramedic took Mihailovna by the arm.

"Come on love, you'll have to move now, we need to get her out of there."

Strong arms enfolded Gaffy and steered her away from the carnage toward the stunned faces of the onlookers.

The ambulance men tried to move Ella.

"No good mate, she's trapped between them, better be quick about this, she's losing blood and fading fast here, looks like the rib cage is crushed and the lungs are filling up. Get the doc over here now."

Gaffy fought off everyone and screamed at the rescuers to get Ella out, why were they waiting? An officer tried his best to calm her, explaining that Ella was trapped by her right arm, they were struggling he said to keep her alive, they thought it best to remove the arm, it was faster he said.

Hysteria overtook Gaffy, she fought and screamed at them, clawed them like a wildcat,

"You, you can't, oh God no, you can't, she___ she___ she's too___it's too important, she, she's an artist, oh God no, don't let them do this, you, you have to save her, save IT, please, oh God please."

"I'm going to remove the hand, it's partially off already, get that morphine into her, keep that torch on the area, it's hard to see with so much blood and keep that bloody woman back, but soon as we've left, get whatever there is left, bag it in the cooler and follow. We might be able to reattach, best I can do, but I think it will be too damaged."

A sudden calm and a cold clamminess descended on Gaffy. Her eyes stared bleakly from her skull as she instructed her secretary with a strident urgency.

"I'm going with her, get hold of Sir George Stevenson and get hold of Pippa, now, do it now, get them to wherever they take her."

Chapter Twenty Eight

Sir George Stevenson was just about to retire for the night when the frantic call from Mihailovna's team reached him. He was the official surgeon to Her Majesty the Queen and had in fact treated Mihailovna and many other sports personalities in the past. A mild-mannered, rotund man in his early sixties he had always kept abreast of new techniques and treatments and commanded a great deal of respect amongst his peers and the public.

Mihailovna and Pippa Adams were waiting for him on his arrival at St. Cuthbert's. Mihailovna's grey cotton sweats and cheeks were besmirched with her own and Ella's blood; she sat hunched, rocking to and fro, tearing at her hair and muttering to herself in Russian. She was praying, in the only language, she knew how to.

Stevenson nodded to Pippa and gently laid his hand on Mihailovna's shoulder before leaving to seek a doctor and find out what the full extent of the damage to Ella Michaels was.

When he returned he quietly told Mihailovna that Ella had been stabilized, a rib had punctured the lung, narrowly missing the heart, she was critical but they were doing all that they could, the hand and part of the forearm had been reattached temporarily but there was little hope, the damage was extensive. He shook his head sadly.

Mihailovna started at his words and clutched frantically at him.

"You don't understand Sir George, this can't happen, you have to fix it."

She turned her hot, red-rimmed pleading eyes on Pippa.

"Do something, do it now, show him____ we have to show him."

Chapter Twenty Nine

In the gloom of the night, the tall buildings of the London streets became like canyons and the street lighting barely cut through the darkness as Mihailovna and Sir George Stevenson stood waiting on the Tate Gallery steps Gaffy struggled to stop her teeth from chattering as her body was wracked with convulsions. Sir George wrapped her in his arms, holding her tight to him till the shuddering sobs subsided; he was aware that she was in shock and didn't fully understand why they were here. The night was still and they listened as hollow footsteps approached them. The door opened and they were quietly admitted.

Shortly before their arrival the chief security officer on the night watch, Jack Miller, had received a call from the directors informing him to admit them and accompany them to the exhibits. He had been told to keep a sharp eye on them, listen carefully and report back immediately.

They walked through the dimly lit corridors and entered the main gallery where the sculptures stood, silent sentinels, who howled their testimony to the genius of the hands that had formed them.

Mihailovna had never been to see them, she had intended to, had been impressed by the pictures in the brochures but nothing had quite prepared her for this. Now she stood before them gazing in awe, as they stood, her static accusers of the horror that she had wrought.

"My God. They are beautiful"

Pain swelled in her chest, her eyes filled and voiceless grief overwhelmed her.

"Yes, they are. Magnificent," Sir George acquiesced, his voice low, reverent, muted by the passion and emotion that he saw within them.

"I see now," He said, "perhaps there is a chance, there has to be. I can think of only one man, Chinese. Dr. Chen Lo. I have met him, microsurgery, his field. He has made massive inroads if anyone can do it maybe him. I'll talk to him; get him here as soon as possible. I'm sure he will want to try when he has seen these. We'll email photos, anything, I'll see to it right away."

A glimmer of hope lodged itself within Mihailovna's heart.

When they had left the gallery Jack Miller called his directors and reported all that they had said.

"Let's hope we can keep a lid on this, especially with the 'dike' involved." Sir Hugh Carrington said in his plum pompous tones to his fellow directors on their conference call.

"Are you mad man, the prices will rocket, we already have serious money offers, this will send them through the roof, we're talking astronomical figures here and our percentage___. Think of the publicity, the crowds we will draw in." George Seymour always had his eye on the money.

"It is totally unethical, we can't"

"WE won't."

An hour later, "OK Jack, as we discussed, let loose the dogs of war."

"Sir?" Jack asked in consternation, not fully understanding the reference.

"News 'hounds' Jack, hounds, they'll soon pick up the scent and run with it." Seymour chuckled to himself.

Jack Miller put in his calls to the popular tabloids informing them of the unusualness of his night visitors. It did not take long for the newshounds to cobble together a story based on a few facts and a good deal of speculation since none of the main players were talking but there was always someone, someone on the periphery who would.

Chapter Thirty

The first story appeared the next morning with pictures of Mihailovna and a photo frame of Ella Michaels taken from a film of Wimbledon where she had been sitting in the spectator's seats.

TETE AU TATE

WHAT WERE THE QUEEN OF WIMBLEDON AND THE QUEEN'S OWN SURGEON DOING TOURING THE TATE GALLERY IN THE MIDDLE OF THE NIGHT

Speculation has been rife throughout Wimbledon fortnight as to just who the mystery lady in the Champion's entourage is. The answer is Ella Michaels, a British sculptor, whose first exhibition just opened at the Tate Gallery, to rave reviews. The sculptor has been present in the player's box throughout most of the tournament and it certainly did appear that Mihailovna was playing specifically for the woman. Mihailovna's semi-final glitch where she bravely fought her way back from one set down was thought to be the result of the absence of Michaels and sparked interest as to what exactly the relationship was between the two women.

The Tate Gallery is heralding Ella Michaels as the new 'Master' of the age. There is no doubt that the sculptures are a work of genius and have already attracted enormous interest and high bids from worldwide collectors have already been received for the ensuing auction. Prices are expected to rocket now since Ella Michaels was last night involved in a vehicular accident along with joyriders and local police, and sustained serious chest and right arm injuries.

The arm was amputated from mid-forearm down at the scene of the accident. Rumour has it that Michaels left the rented property of Mihailovna in haste after a lover's tiff resulting in physical violence with Mihailovna sustaining some facial and neck bruising. An onlooker observed Mihailovna and the young Jana Djochevnic in a 'clinch' when Michaels arrived on the scene. 'I thought she was going to kill her.' They said when Michaels had attacked Mihailovna. The fracas was broken up and Michaels drove off the property at considerable speed and straight into the path of a vehicle fleeing from the police. There is some speculation that Michaels had been smoking cannabis though this is as yet unconfirmed.

Hospital reports say that Michaels is now stable but severe damage to the right hand and arm of the sculptor looks set to ensure that there will be no more works of art. Sir George Stevenson, the Queen's own surgeon was summoned to the Tate Gallery by Mihailovna, another of his esteemed patients and there is speculation that attempts will be made to reattach the arm and hand using microsurgery, though professional sources view their undertaking as an almost impossible task, in light of the extensive trauma sustained.

Chapter Thirty One

Sir George's driver had collected Chen Lo from the airport. Lo was a short unassuming man, the large round spectacles he wore gave him an owlish appearance, his clipped speech and mincing walk giving evidence of his meticulousness. He declined the offer of going straight to the hotel to freshen up but chose rather to visit the Tate Gallery first and from there went straight to St. Cuthbert's.

"Horrendous, so many reporter. Sir George, please, the x-rays."

Chen Lo waived off Sir George's effusive thanks, his manner crisp, abrupt but immeasurably polite and spent some time poring over the x-rays and charts before asking to see his patient. On their walk to Ella's private room, he confirmed theatre arrangements and the use of a team of surgeons including Sir George to assist him.

"Madam Michaels, I am most honored to meet with you," Lo bowed and took Ella's undamaged hand gently into his own. "I have seen your momentous work. I do not speculate that I can make full restoration, but I am here to make every effort if you would be pleased to allow me the honor. What we undertake will not be accomplished in one operation, we must be very patient. Tomorrow morning when I am refreshed, with Sir George's team's assistance we will begin our journey."

Sir George remained behind for a moment, "Thank you, Sir George." Ella's voice croaked with the exertion of speaking as she labored for breath.

"Thank Mihailovna, she would like to see you, she has not left here since the accident."

At the mention of Gaffy's name, Ella turned her face to the wall, "Tell her to go, please." She whispered.

Crystal watched as Mihailovna spoke quietly with Sir George, her shoulders slumped and she seemed to crumple into his arms. He led her away towards the rear of the hospital to avoid the circus of reporters gathering hungrily.

Chapter Thirty Two

For twelve hours Chen Lo and the team of surgeons worked fastidiously on the replanted arm and hand, restoring blood flow through arteries and veins, rebuilding the bony skeleton, pinning the broken finger and hand bones together and connecting tendons and nerves as required, repairing torn ligaments and grafting skin. When the hand turned pink and the pulse was restored in the wrist the first step on a long road to recovery was finished.

Lo turned to Sir George as they stripped off the masks and gloves, "I fear the damage to the thumb and forefinger is so extensive that we cannot repair this but I have some ideas, we can go down two different roads, one we can rebuild, using the great toe this is replacement and two there is transplantation perhaps a better option cosmetically but more difficult to find the spare part that matches. I have some contacts and will investigate these areas more fully before we decide to continue with the next stage. We cannot know my friend at this moment, but we can pray to whatever Gods we have. Please to join me for dinner this evening at my very pleasant hotel where I intend to enjoy some of your wonderful Scotch whiskey, tomorrow I shall leave and I shall return in six weeks. Please to ensure that full care is taken to keep the hand immobile and protected at all costs."

Sir George nodded his assent, "You went then to the Tate first?"

"I wished to see for myself; my air ticket was paid for by Jian Arts, Jian is a Chinese word you know, it's meaning a little obscure but perhaps close to the translation, 'ultimate creator'. Also, we know Miss Michaels; our government has had some dealings with her in the past. We must do all that is possible."

Chen Lo returned to Beijing the next day accompanied by a crate of Sir George's finest Scotch whiskey.

Chapter Thirty Three

Crystal sat beside her brother in their mother's private room, their hands clasped tightly, the skin stretched taut across their knuckles, "It'll be okay Jazz, I'm sure, Mummy is strong, she'll get through this."

Jasper was Ella's second child, twenty-two years old, tall at 6'2" with an athletic build. He was dark-haired like his sister but paler in coloring and his features mirrored his mother's. He had gained a double first in chemistry at Strathclyde but putting his own career aside had now taken over the running of Jian Arts for the time being to give his mother the freedom needed to sculpt. Both children had remained with their mother throughout their childhood and neither had ever referred to each other as half siblings. They trusted and respected their mother, had never kept secrets from one another and had been able to discuss any aspects of their lives amongst themselves, giving rise to their consummate closeness.

Jasper felt the sting of tears and grimaced as he tried to swallow the bile rising acidly into his throat making it hard for him speak as he stared at his mother's right arm and hand. It appeared Frankensteinian to him, the blue-black skin stained with a yellowish antiseptic paint, crisscrossed with untidy stitching. The cage surrounding the swollen limb was like an evil instrument of torture, metal rods with butterfly screws pierced the arm and wrist and smaller versions still, protruded from several of the fingers. "How do we know, even they don't know?"

"Mummy doesn't know yet about the stories in the press. Adam has arranged a helicopter from the heliport here, we'll go out through the roof, when the time comes, but we have to let her know something of what is going on I suppose, but she'll take it very hard."

As Ella stirred, Jasper cradled her gently and held the iced water to her dry lips. "It's okay Mum, its okay, we're here. Dr. Lo and Sir George think it went well." He tried to quell his growing horror at what he surmised would be his mother's own when she saw her injuries more fully and the results of the surgery.

They broke the news of the press spectacle and the resulting spate of robberies, thefts of limited edition sculptures by Ella and the clamor of those who tried for high prices on the internet. They were as tactful as they could be but Ella was devastated that so much could have happened, as a result of her fit of rage and that it could have caused such further tragedy to erupt. She was overwhelmed by despair and the doctor felt it best she be kept sedated for a few days and as she drifted into blessed oblivion she asked only once of Mihailovna to be told that she had left with Sir George and forced from Crystal a promise that she would go home to Matt and Xenon, Jasper would stay with her until she could leave with him and Adam.

Chapter Thirty Four

Crystal walked up to the bar in the White Swan and ordered herself a Coke and a single malt for Adam, "Hello, mi duck how's your mom?" asked the landlord as he poured the drinks.

"No change, Tony, thanks. As if the accident wasn't enough for her to cope with, she has all this. This lot, all this fuss, reporters camping out at the hospital, hounding me and Jazz for information, it's a fucking crime."

Pete Dennison was a hardened criminal who had spent twelve of his thirty-five years inside. He stood, five foot nine with a slim well-muscled body, sporting various amateur prison tattoos, his wizened features were topped by a shaven head and large protruding ears. As he propped up the bar he slowly sipped at his bitter, Ruddles County, a rather flat but strong real ale, and tuned in to other customer's conversations. He was on the alert for any useful information, as he waited for his two associates who were reconnoitering the surrounding villages. Housebreaking was their game and in the main, they were on the lookout for any country house properties that could afford them rich pickings paintings, antiques etcetera, especially if the houses were unoccupied.

"What about her hand, will it get better?" Tony asked sadly.

"There really is no way of telling and even if it does it is going to be a really long haul, it's so tragic."

"I don't suppose all this speculation about what the sculptures are worth, helps. The papers say there have been several robberies already of some of her limited edition pieces plus folk jumping on the bandwagon and offering them for sale. You'd better watch out, what with that piece she did for Xenon's christening. Christ, it must be worth a small fortune."

"Well we would never sell it anyway so we'll never know."

"Any ow duck, give her our love, and tell her we're thinking on er, won't you? That's on the house." He nodded.

"Thanks, Tony, we'll pass on the message," Crystal promised and she went to sit nearby with Adam Fergusson and continued her conversation quietly with him.

Charles Warrender answered his mobile to find an excited, keyed up Dennison on the line.

"You'll never guess what I've stumbled across Warrender, right down your street this. That sculptress her that's injured that's in all the papers, that Ellen McKiles, her daughter lives here, and guess what else, she's got a sculpture, by her mother, in her house."

"You mean Ella Michaels?"

"Yeah! That's the one."

"What exactly is the setup? Can you get access?"

"I'll let you know, find out any interest, and we'll talk money."

Chapter Thirty Five

Lights out, the truck coasted silently and came to a stop alongside the rear of the property. Three men, clothed in black and wearing balaclavas moved stealthily to the kitchen door. One of them attached a rubber sucker to the pane and carefully cut out a circle of glass, removed it and reached inside to release the bolt.

They had been watching the house for several days, taking careful notes of the owner's comings and goings and Dennison was fairly certain no one would disturb them. Using torches they made their way through the kitchen and dining room, finally arriving in a large sitting room where they found what they were looking for.

"Matt and Xenon are still at his Mum's until tomorrow, we thought it best to keep him out of the public eye, too many reporters hanging around. I've been busy at the stables what with the new foal but Adam has taken over now so I shall try to catch up with some sleep and you should try to get some rest Mummy, try not to dwell on things too much. Jazz and Adam will be there to bring you home tomorrow and I'll see you when you get here, love you lots, and lots and lots." Crystal blew kisses into her mobile, pressed the close button and inserted the key into the front door. All three men's heads turned towards the sound.

"Shite!" Dennison hissed through his teeth, "Quick, behind the door," he signaled, with the heavy torch, "whack whoever it is with this if they come in here." Crystal went down the long hall straight to the kitchen, lit only by the dim glow of an overhead light thrown on to the central island, where she tossed her bag and car keys with a sigh, and turning to a kitchen cabinet took out a bottle of brandy and a glass. I need a drink she thought kneading her forehead with her fingers and attempting to massage away the gathering tension. Her hand trembled slightly as she lifted the glass to her lips and drank deeply, her thoughts on her mother, how she would cope in this gathering storm. As the burn of the alcohol slid down her throat, Tony's words in the pub a few days before came back to her and she was overcome with a sudden desire to look again at the sculpture that he had mentioned. There's hope she thought smiling to herself and carried the drink into the sitting room.

As Crystal flicked the switch and light flared into the room, Dennison snatched back the heavy metal torch and swung it hard into the back of her skull.

Chapter Thirty Six

Matt stared at Crystal's lifeless body with disbelief. How could she be dead she just seemed asleep, There had been no blood, nothing ghastly to warn him, to prepare him for the shock of the chill of her body as he had touched her. Her olive skin had a grayish hue and her lips a blue tinge.

He was still in the same position, holding Crystal in his arms, when the ambulance and police had arrived, still trying futilely to instill warmth into her limp body, ignoring the cries and bewilderment of his small son. The doctor and ambulance crew had pried them apart, telling him they would take care of her now. Matt had sat stunned incapable of physical movement as his brain diverted all energy to thought processes in an attempt to come to terms with the reality of what had happened. First, the ambulance men, and police and finally the Scene of Crimes Officers had roamed the house in their white hooded overalls, their feet clad in the white papery overshoes. Their appearance was surreal to Matt like that of overgrown babies in romper suits. A policewoman had tried to comfort the small boy, who failed to understand his father's aloofness and his mother's enduring stillness.

Several officers and the doctor had tried to talk to him to ply him with tea, something stronger, but nothing had penetrated the cocoon into which he had withdrawn. An officer had steered him from the house to a waiting car. Adam Fergusson had called Matt's mother Jean who had come immediately and taken her son and grandson back to her home.

"She must have walked in on them; do we know what was taken?"

"Yes sir, Fergusson, he lives just down the road in the Lodge house, he says it was a sculpture. The victim is Ella Michaels' daughter."

"No fucking wonder there's so many press here. Just one blow looks like. Medical Examiner thinks it's a brain stem injury, heavy blunt instrument to the medulla or something, anyway we'll know more after the autopsy. Where is he, this Fergusson?"

"Left a short while ago in a helicopter, gone to pick up the mother from the hospital."

"Did SOCO get anything?"

"Not much sir, gloves it looks like, professional job, knew what they wanted, in and out 'cept they obviously weren't expecting anyone here. Still, we've officers canvassing the area, let's hope somebody saw something."

Adam Fergusson had indeed flown to St. Cuthbert's in the helicopter and it was with a dull ache in his chest that he had brooded how to tell Ella of her daughter's murder and just what the repercussions, on her already fragile state of mind, may be.

Ella began making low animal sounds in her throat, barely articulate, an almost primitive sound. She started to speak but could only manage a sort of dragged out stuttering word, "No, no, no," Ella began shaking like someone freezing, she gulped at the air like a drowning woman, and then the tears came in deep, shuddering, choking sobs that seemed interminable. Ella's heart had seemed to stop as her mind closed over Adam's words, he clung to her hand, offering a mooring line in her churning sea of grief until like water over stones dropped into a fathomless pool blissful unconsciousness embraced her.

Jasper's pain was evident as he struggled to contain his agony, his voice hoarse with crying as he asked Adam, "What did we do, what did any of us do to deserve all this? My mother will never recover, never get over this. Sir George says she's shut down, not responding at all to anything. I don't know what to do, how to help."

"Alright son, it'll be alright." Adam's arms enfolded the tall strong young man as though he were a child, pressing his face into the rough tweed of his jacket. "You go now, Matt needs you right now and that wee boy, there's a good deal te sort out and you'll be better busying yourself. I'll no leave your mother, have nay fear of that. She'll pull through this, her mind is just resting." He patted Jasper's shoulder, "Go now, and take the 'copter we'll be there in a few days or more, soon as she finds her way back, from wherever it is she's slipped away te."

Chapter Thirty Seven

Ella was encased in a full-length black cashmere Mansfield coat. The fine bones of her features sharper, her eyes more sunken, still smudged beneath with purple bruising, worry lines etched her forehead and the hair beneath the black silk scarf was lackluster but though she seemed to Adam Fergusson to lack substance, to have gained a shrunken fragility, she visibly drew herself together, her backbone ramrod straight as she looked to both him and Sir George.

"I want to go there first, to the Tate; I want to see them again. I have to know what to do to stop this from going any further, no one else must be hurt by this."

"It's late, they'll be closing we'll nay get there in time t'day."

"I must go. I have to."

Sir George interceded, "If you must, take my car and driver, I'll phone ahead and stay with the helicopter.

In the shelter of the back of Sir George's car, Adam leaned into Ella, raising the already high collar of the coat, to partly cover her face and set his sunglasses on her nose. "There's a crowd." He said softly.

As Fergusson and Ella approached the monumental edifice of the Tate Gallery, their passage on the steps was blocked by some twenty or so students arguing their right to enter. Their impassioned pleas that the bus had broken down on the motorway, they couldn't help the delay and this was their only chance, the sculptures would be gone soon, they couldn't come back, all fell on deaf ears. Adam pressed his way forward, leading Ella and as they arrived at the head of the queue she spoke in a whisper to him. Forging ahead Adam took the arm of the security guard and commanded, "Let them in, ye have to stay open fer us, so let them through, Ms. Michaels' orders man." Jack Millar was beset with guilt, he struggled with his conscience for only a moment before throwing open the doors and admitting the students.

The still silence of the gallery was broken by the awed murmurs of the youngsters as they moved amongst the exhibits, gesticulating enthusiastically.

Ella lingered gazing at her most loved piece of work, Prisoners of Passion, and Adam stepped back, turning aside to allow her this private moment. The awesome bronze sculpture of the pair of lovers stood larger than life-size encircled, roped off from the public. Gingerly Ella stepped over the white rope barrier and reaching out lovingly caressed its' gleaming bronze surface. Blistering tears nettled her eyes as she felt the warmth of its' metal rise into her whole being, visions of her laughing Crystal sparkled across her mind as lightning flashed across thunderous skies. A five-year-old Crystal with a chocolate smeared mouth, tense with concentration, tongue between her small white even teeth, a packet of chocolate drops grasped in one hand and in her other small fist an Island of Lewis chess piece as she struggled to grasp the complex moves of the game. Crystal danced on; Ella closed her eyes on the phantom and a teardrop splashed onto the bronze figures.

"You can't do that, you're not allowed to touch them." The strident tones of the young man ceased abruptly as Fergusson jumped to attention, his arm grasping the jacket of the boy and jerking him back from Ella viciously. Ella had raised her arm in defense and the boy's eyes fell on the ugly cage encasing her right arm and hand. "Oh God, I'm sorry, I'm so sorry. It's you, it's really you." He stammered reverentially.

"Adam, please, it's alright, leave him."

The boy though would not be quieted by Fergusson, now he called his discovery excitedly to his fellow students and panic flashed momentarily across Ella's gaunt face as they clamored for her attention.

Adam growled at them, "Can ye no see the pain she's in, fer the love of God, give her space, will yez."

A young girl stepped forward, her body all improbable angles, her pale translucent skin a stark contrast to her eyes heavy with mascara, bright with tears, and her egg-plant painted slash of a mouth.

"We came all the way from Manchester. Nearly didn't let us in. I'm so sorry___so sorry___ but we'll never have another chance, no one will. When they are sold, they'll be gone into private collections all we'll be left will be pictures. Not the same." The other students murmured their assent.

After listening to the youngsters for a half hour and not knowing whether her hand would ever be capable of reproducing such works again, maybe never she thought and felt the loss deep within, but again an image of Crystal smiling skipped behind her eyes and Ella thought she knew what was necessary.

"Thank you; I know now what to do. You are right, they shouldn't be sold."

"Seriously, would you do that? They're priceless anyway, surely? What with the ___ "

Callous youth, thought Ella, as the boy tossed back his unruly thatch of red blonde hair revealing a face that was pale behind its' constellation of freckles Ella finished for him "No, not priceless," she paused, "the price has already been paid," and in a hushed aside to Fergusson, "maybe some of this madness will stop if I do this," her voice betrayed the depths of her melancholy.

PART THREE

Chapter Thirty Eight

Charles Warrender picked up the trilling phone on his ornate mahogany desk and listened as Dennison pleaded.

"You said you had an offer, a million was the price."

"That was before you killed an innocent young woman, you bloody fool."

"It weren't me." Dennison lied, "It was Charlie, eavy anded git. He just meant to knock her out, it were an accident."

"Whatever. The news reports are full of the idea that the hand will be repaired. The Chinese surgeon says given a series of operations to repair nerve damage etcetera that sufficient feeling will be restored. My buyers are no fools, the other sculptures have been withdrawn from sale but they'll bide their time and wait for the final outcome before making an offer now."

"The fucking thing is hot," Dennison gasped, "I need to get away, and the fucking cops are throwing everything they've got at this."

"Get out now Dennison, ferry to France, I'll send a man with some cash, a couple of hundred thousand, for now, be ready for him, have the sculpture transported to my warehouse and clear everything up that might show any connection to me and get as far away as you can."

Warrender tweaked the cuffs of his dark pin-striped Armani suit fingered his heavy gold cuff links and leaned back in the deep leather upholstered chair. He had finely chiseled features, his light sunbed tan trim waist and broad shoulders were those of someone who worked out regularly. His urbane elegance had a contrived unctuous quality as he flicked the shock of fair hair from his forehead in a habitual gesture. Warrender smiled to himself though the smile never reached his eyes, making it more the rapacious leer of a wolf. He lifted his mobile and made the following call.

"Dennison is waiting for you now and according to the newspapers you have six weeks before the next operation on the woman, but speed will ensure that no one will be aware of the threat at this moment. No cordon of protection is in place. You have your targets."

Chapter Thirty Nine

Packer closed the mobile and ground it underfoot. His florid unlined complexion; his ginger hair shaved close to his skull gave at first glimpse the impression of a babyface but a glance from those arctic, blue-green eyes reminded one of a predator and soon dispelled the image of any innocence. He looked through the contents of the brown envelope once more, betraying not a single emotion as he fixed the image of the woman and the detailed brief in his mind; he tore them into fragments setting them alight in the ashtray and watched patiently as they burned. He scooped the ashes along with the remains of the phone into a black bin liner and checking the contents of his large leather hold-all; it contained a long, bolt-action rifle, a Rank-Pullin, starlight scope, chambering 22 magnum subsonic rounds, an assassin's gun, he hefted both, left the cheap hotel room and climbed into a nondescript green Volvo estate, its' number plates partially obscured by the same mud that was splattered along its' sides,

Parking the Volvo on the concrete car park Packer approached the old brick-built warehouse, stepping purposefully through rain puddles, broken glass crunching under the soles of his soft leather combat boots. The building looked unused, its brickwork in need of re-pointing, the multi-paned windows, many cracked and broken were dark and uninviting. Outside the door, he fitted the silencer to the SIG-SAUER P220 semi-automatic pistol, dropped his hand behind his back and gave the requisite knock to signal his arrival.

The door opened a crack and a head peered out cautiously. Packer entered, following behind Jackson, one of Dennison's minions, he lightly tapped him on the shoulder. As Jackson turned to face Packer, he raised the pistol and shot him between the eyes, catching the body as it slumped forward and lowering it gently to the floor. An Aladdin's Cave greeted him inside. The floors were strewn with several open wooden crates, polystyrene and paper packing materials and stacked around the walls were paintings and antique furniture galore. A wooden staircase led up to a dimly lit office, its glass windows overlooking the floor area. Packer took the stairs two at a time with feline grace.

"Good, here you are, got the money, and where's Jackson?"

"Following me, did the sculpture get off to Warrender?"

"Yeh, here look."

Packer scanned the documents swiftly and satisfied, raised the pistol and shot Dennison and his assistant. He stepped close to their bodies and felt for a pulse. Nothing. He went back down the staircase and in a small storeroom found what he needed. Partially filled old paint cans, oily rags and turpentine provided him with enough accelerant and piling them into a heap and scattering the rest amidst the furnishings he methodically set alight to the warehouse. Outside he sat in the car until he was certain that the fire had a good hold before driving away.

Chapter Forty

They stopped at the Chapel of Rest, at the funeral home. Adam made a move to accompany Ella as she approached the black lacquered casket but was stayed by Jasper's hand.

"Give her a moment of privacy."

It's said that the organ of the heart has no capacity to feel emotions yet Ella felt as though a great stone was lying in her chest making it difficult to breathe. She looked down at Crystal's beautiful face, her gaze fixed, so still now that life had gone, her expression blank and inanimate. She felt empty, something had gone from her. The tears fell softly down her cheeks; her hand reached out and brushed Crystal's face gently.

"Good-bye darling, she whispered. "I love you."

Dense bushes, trees and a low wall shielded Packer from sight. He crouched unmoving in the undergrowth surrounding Kesteven Park's car park, his muscles cramped a little but he ignored them, his years as a sniper in the forces having trained him well for long periods of stillness. Packer had scoped the position the night before; the park was some 400 yards from his target, separated by the low wall and tree line and just a few yards from the parked Volvo, its' door hanging open in readiness.

Warrender was right he thought as the funeral cortege pulled slowly in front of the long low beige brick building that housed the crematorium, no protection. He adjusted his focus to the clear area alongside the building, The Garden of Remembrance and settled down again to wait.

Jasper had made the necessary funeral arrangements; his brother-in-law Matt still seemed unable to grasp the finality of his wife's death. The ceremonies had been somber and short a mercy to those in attendance with their all too visible grief and pain. The small party emerged from a side entrance into the Garden of Remembrance, the lounging pack of journalists and photographers sprang to life. Fergusson and Jasper tried to shield Ella Michaels from the waiting press. Fergusson bent his face close to one reporter with a vulturine swoop his eyes projecting a laser of contempt.

"Fuck off will yers, give the family a break." he hissed through clenched teeth.

Packer found his target in the crosshairs of the scope, breathed in and as he released the breath, lightly squeezed the trigger.

One reporter jostled forward using his bulk to press his advantage, his camera raised high above the heads of the others, he called Ella's name and as she turned her head to him, momentarily stunned by the flash, his face exploded, a red mist clouded her eyes as a mass of blood, bone and brains sprayed across her. For a moment they seemed as figures frozen in a tableau vivant before Fergusson threw himself across Ella, bringing them both to a jarring thud as they made contact with the gravel of the walkway. He dragged her with him into the shelter of the doorway and then eased her urgently through the door and back inside the crematorium. Pandemonium reigned outside as people ran for cover but there were no more shots.

"Fucking shite, shite, shite," mouthed Packer angrily, gathering up the rifle and the shell casing he moved swiftly back to his Volvo tossing the weapon into the passenger well alongside him he gunned the engine and screamed out of the car park.

Jane Dee Simpson "Prisoners of our own device"

An eerie silence descended upon the garden and the coppery tang

of blood replaced the heady scent of the funeral flowers.

Chapter Forty One

The long table in the dining room was laden with untouched food, the few people who had come back to the house milled around aimlessly, their black-clad figures like wraiths, their faces stricken, their eyes wide, numbed with shock. Matt poured himself a brandy with shaking hands. Jasper sat beside his mother cradling her head in his hands.

"How is she?" Asked the Inspector.

"Nae bloody good, that's for sure, that bullet was meant for her."

"Let's go into the library where we can talk," Adam said quietly.

"No doubt about it. We've been looking for a guy seen in the area about the time of Crystal's murder name of Dennison a known villain but he's been keeping a low profile. We got word that he had a warehouse down in London but when the Met went to check it out it had burned to the ground and what we presume was his body was identified this morning along with two others, burned up in the fire in London, but all three were shot first."

"Professional?"

"Oh yes, Art and Antiques are on to it, they may sound like rather a benign squad, a bunch of professors with badges but what they do is no joking matter. The black market in art spreads worldwide and is linked up with organized crime along the way. People get hurt, currencies range from Van Gogh's to Kalashnikovs to heroin and people get killed.

I'd say it was the same shooter as today. There have been thefts of some of the small limited edition pieces and there is still some trading going on both legal and illegal with high prices being demanded. The Jian company has ceased trading in any of her work which helps and since the statement in the press that Ms. Michaels intends to cede the sculptures in the exhibition to the National Gallery on permanent loan, the stolen one from her daughter is the only major one out there and whoever has it has decided to up the ante by making sure there are never any more. We've officers in place outside, he'll not get through immediately but this is a quiet place with lots of lands around for cover, it may well be best to move her to a safe house."

Fergusson deliberated on the problem for an hour or so before making several hushed phone calls to former colleagues then together with Jasper a plan was formulated and the two of them argued it through with Ella before putting it into action.

Packer was perched high in a tree in the woods watching the house through high powered binoculars when he heard the loud thrumming of the helicopter blades approach and its' giant blue dragonfly shape descend behind the house. He watched for an hour only to see the helicopter take off again, his prey had escaped he presumed, destination unknown. As he checked his maps for the closest airfield, Humberside, some thirty miles away, he guessed the helicopter may have come from there and sped off in that direction.

Humberside airport was very small, few flights left there anymore and with discrete inquiries and a little bribery he managed to ascertain that the helicopter had indeed landed there a short while ago the party of four onboard though had transferred immediately to a Lear Jet that had been fully fuelled and standing by. No one was prepared to tell him its' destination if they, in fact, were even aware

of it.

Chapter Forty Two

Galataria was a small village nestling in the foothills of the Troodos Mountains. 650 meters above sea level 35 kilometers from Paphos and 6 kilometers from Panagia, the birthplace of Archbishop Makarios, in Cyprus. The tiny hamlet set in the wine region of the island consisted of around one hundred or so old stone-built homes, a small factory making feta, halloumi cheese, and other grape products and one winery, it had no bars or tavernas, not even a shop only a small coffee shop to service a community of mainly farmers, few youngsters and seldom any visitors.

The village was picturesque in an austere way, the locals passed their time working the land and sitting in the dappled sunlight beneath the shade of a pomegranate and a fig tree in the tiny unpaved square of dirt that passed for a patio outside the coffee shop, the men playing cards and backgammon and the women, splitting beans or shelling nuts for the local delicacy shuzuko, a grape jelly sausage containing whatever nuts were seasonal.

Life meandered in Galataria, with the slow tranquility of a ponderous, sluggish river.

Chapter Forty Three

Four people emerged from the Lear Jet at Paphos airport, Kerry Styles, Jim Boyle, Fergusson, and Ella Michaels. Styles and Boyle were ex SAS now running their own private security firm Sentinel and old colleagues of Fergusson. Protection for the famous was the meat of their business, they were expensive but in Fergusson's mind, you got what you paid for. Fergusson had called the security firm, Sentinel from Ella's home and been answered by an anonymous operator.

"This is Adam Fergusson; Jim Boyle is an old friend and gave me this number to call when times are difficult."

There was a hiss and click as Fergusson was transferred to a secure line.

"Hello, Mr. Fergusson what is the nature of your emergency."

"Life and death."

"Is the danger imminent?"

"Yes, there have been five deaths already. We are insecure."

Fergusson gave the operator his requirements and their location and was told that Boyle and another operative would arrive in one hour by helicopter and to be ready to move almost immediately.

Boyle and Fergusson greeted each other as old friends and then got down to business; Boyle had brought satellite phones which were encrypted, one for Jasper to keep him up to date and one each for the rest of the party. Mobile phones were to be left behind and switched off. When Fergusson had appraised Boyle and Styles fully of the situation Boyle explained that a Lear Jet was waiting at Humberside Airport, they would be met at their final destination with gear bags.

A black BMW pulled alongside them and levered open its' boot. With a cursory glance at the contents, Boyle transferred two large metal cases along with their sparse luggage to the waiting long wheel based Range Rover kept on the island by Adam. They climbed aboard and making one short stop to collect any necessary food supplies continued with their journey. Their ears popped as the vehicle started to climb through the darkness along narrow twisting roads, their destination, Galataria.

Adam Fergusson had served in Cyrus before the Turkish/Cypriot troubles and had a long-standing love affair with the island and its people. Twenty years earlier he had bought the old stone farmhouse with its vineyard and olives, placed some 2 kilometers from Galataria. Over the twenty years, Fergusson had learned to speak Greek Cypriot, the land and house were well maintained by a neighboring couple in his absences, the villagers were fond of him and used to the eccentricities and idiosyncrasies of the tacit Scotsman. They left him well alone but still were happy to see him whenever he felt the need for their company and Adam had made the house his bolt-hole, a place he went to commune with nature and share the simplicity of the villagers' lives.

Solar lights flared brightly lighting the long driveway to the stone-built house. Stark white gravel crunched under the huge wheels, and a harsh electronic buzz signaled the opening of the wrought iron gates, they whined as they swung wide and closed with a metallic clang as they swallowed the vehicle.

Chapter Forty Four

The original house now the ground floor was built of multi-hued stone walls about a foot in thickness, keeping the house cool in summer and warm in the winter months. Weathered small pale green shuttered windows ran along the length of the building. An upper storey of white stucco with a red corrugated tiled roof had been added later and surrounded by a wooden balcony in the same pale green paintwork. The balcony extended over the tiled area in front of the house and was dripping with clusters of fat green grapes. Two steps down from the patio was a low door, and as Adam stooped to enter he cautioned.

"Mind your heads now everyone, these doors were nay built for folk of our height."

They entered into a surprisingly large high ceilinged room the ceiling itself consisted of honey-colored bamboo canes laid tightly alongside each other, and secured by thick rustic round poles then supported by one great wooden beam down the length of the room. This beam, in turn, was held up by three more substantial polished tree trunks roped together top and bottom and mounted on a plinth in the center of the room. The two parallel stone walls were abridged by two of white plaster at each end which were decorated with large canvases whose vivid visceral colors and forceful, confident brushwork spoke of violence in two dimensions. The room was dominated by a massive stone fireplace at one end, had a pale cream highly polished marble floor and was tastefully furnished with large worn leather sofas, a large heavy coffee table, smaller matching side tables, and a mahogany slatted wooden rug from Thailand in front of the fire. Heavy dark wood antiques formed a dining area behind them where Adam stopped to light ten large yellowish fat candles on a walnut sofa table, The candles were arrayed on a long polished wooden platter with round scooped indentations which he informed his visitors was in fact normally used for curing the dough when making bread.

They dropped their luggage on the floor and Styles carried the food into a smallish but well-equipped country kitchen. Fergusson followed her in suggesting a drink to relax them all and proceeded to open a dark dusty bottle of what was obvious by the label, his own wine. Pointing out to Styles a cupboard containing fine crystalware he piled a large plate with feta cheese, grapes, tomatoes, olives, and bread and carried them back into the great room.

"Let's relax, I'll show you all to your rooms shortly, it's a bit quirky, the house has only two bedrooms but outside in the courtyard are another couple of rooms and a wet room. Many of the houses here you have to go outside to the bedrooms and the kitchen even, but the locals mainly live outside in their courtyards. Ye'll get used to it soon enough."

Ella's face bore the weary signs of the strain of the last few days and unable to cut up her food, she churlishly tossed aside the napkin.

"I can't do this Adam, I need, I need space. I want to be alone for a while."

Fergusson laid a gently restraining hand on her forearm and in a fatherly but commanding voice said, "Easy now hen, sure you're an independent body alright but right now when you need to build your strength. It's no great matter to accept a little help, eat now." And he

poured her wine and cut some bread off the hunk of a loaf for her.

Chapter Forty Five

Fergusson escorted Ella up the open slatted wood staircase in the sitting room along a narrow corridor and into an en suite bedroom. One wall of the room was stone its' soft-hued grays and beiges creating a cool atmosphere. This wall had several stones jutting out into the room on which large church candles were mounted. The flooring was old highly waxed wood and the room housed an ebonized hand-decorated metal four poster bed its head centering the furthest white stucco wall. The bed had a canopy and drapes of light white muslin and was dressed with white Egyptian cotton sheets with a lace edging added here on the island. An old ornate wardrobe and dresser with a heavy gilt mirror and a French 17th-century armchair upholstered in blue and white silk stripes completed the furnishings.

"It's very hot here at the moment; I'd leave the Punkah Walla on if I were you." Fergusson raised his eyes to the center light fitting, brass with a heavy wooden fan beating overhead.

Adam crossed the room and showed Ella the bathroom which with its' large roll-top hydro spa bathtub, state of the art power shower cubical, oval modern ceramic basin set on a polished wooden plinth and ceramic toilet and bidet rather compromised the rustic Cypriot style of the rest of the house. Bamboo towel ladders were draped with plush chocolate and fawn-colored towels, and a small cabinet held an array of toiletries.

"I love the old style but Cypriot plumbing leaves a lot to be desired and I like my comfort." Adam chortled, as he returned to the bedroom and opened the glazed doors to the balcony, smiled and left the bedroom.

Ella struggled to undress using only the one hand and damned the ugly cage under her breath. A cursory wash completed her ablutions and donning a large plush chocolate bathrobe she found hanging on the door, she lit a cigarette and went to sit on one of the balconies two chairs.

The long balcony stretched out over the encompassing darkness like the concourse of a starship on its' voyage through the galaxy, the inky dark sky lit only by a myriad of scintillating stars, a trail of sparkling diamonds scattered across the firmament with the occasional array of fairy lights mirroring them as they sparkled in the surrounding trees. Ella sat musing, breathing in deeply the heady scents of jasmine and honeysuckle assailed her senses. A flashback of her last vision of Mihailovna brought a feeling of nausea and she purposefully dismissed it. She had had little time to assimilate all that had transpired, just a few weeks ago she had been feted at the reception of her open night, a night full of hope and promise then abruptly everything had spun out of control. The death of her beloved Crystal, thoughts of her daughter dispelled the nausea but a sensation of infinite guilt and sadness enveloped her. Someone had tried to kill her and she had had to flee from her home, she was very afraid and she wept silently reflecting on all that had brought her to what seemed like the edge of the world.

Though she had doubted her ability to sleep as she lay down on the bed she was overcome with weariness and the pure still silence of the night soon embraced her in the arms of Morpheus.

Another long stone flat-roofed building across the far end of the courtyard comprised a further two bedrooms, each similarly furnished to that of Ella's and between them a small seating area with sofas and a stone fireplace, two small adjacent buildings housed a modern wet room and a tiny kitchenette. It was here that Boyle and Styles were to be housed and where they sat with Fergusson murmuring in low voices while deciding a plan of action.

They considered themselves safe for the moment, therefore, a good night's sleep was in order. Tomorrow they would walk the perimeter of the land, marking its strengths and its' weak spots and work out a roster of guard duties. Adam explained that the house backed onto an almost sheer earth wall rising some one hundred feet above the rooftops of the outhouses and was fronted by a small vineyard and olive grove before dropping off in a steep incline populated with pine and almond trees to the valley below, apart from the main drive the only access roads were fire breaks requiring a four-wheel-drive vehicle to navigate them. It seemed almost unassailable.

Chapter Forty Six

Ella was woken from a deep sleep by a light knock on the bedroom door and Adam entered carrying a tray with a pot of tea, two cups and saucers, toast and a black plastic rubbish bag, which he placed on the table on the balcony for them.

"Did you sleep?"

"Surprisingly. This is very English, tea and toast, but what's with the bin bag?"

"That my dear is for you," he gestured to his nose and sniffed, "you need to shower." He laughed.

Ella smiled holding up the cage on her arm and raised her eyebrows.

"That's the first smile I've seen from you for days and this here handy contraption along with a rubber band is going to keep the water out and Styles, who for this purpose is thankfully female, is going to help you and you are going to accept her help graciously.   I specifically asked Boyle for a woman for just this situation and someone with some medical skills and Styles fits the bill. She may be a woman, but I am assured by Boyle that she is more than capable in the field. I'm away down to Paphos to phone Sir George and Dr. Lo from a secure phone I could use the satellite phone but we need groceries and whatever medication etcetera Chen Lo may suggest and there's nay shop here."

"Is all this cloak and dagger stuff really necessary?"

"Aye, it is, for the moment we are safe here but in this day and age and with the technology that's out there who knows for how long. Five people are dead already I don't see these people giving up so easily."

With the help of Kerry Styles Ella managed to shower and wash her hair, she had been shocked by her appearance in the mirror. Ella had eaten little to nothing for the past few weeks and her body was emaciated, the shoulder, rib and hip bones protruded from her mottled bruised skin. The thin scar on her forehead and the one circling her chest were both still vivid red lines surrounded by purplish yellow bruising. Kerry had been surprisingly gentle, carefully swabbing dry the flesh around her injuries and Ella had succumbed to her ministrations gratefully. The rest of the morning Ella spent browsing through Adam's bookcase and trying to distract herself with the banality of morning television programs presented by Skye whilst Boyle and Styles heavily armed took turns to patrol outside.

Fergusson contacted Sir George Stevenson and Chen Lo using payphones. Chen Lo was mortified to hear of the attempts on his patient's life and that the peace and tranquility that was necessary for her to heal was not forthcoming and told Fergusson he would, "Ponder on it." Adam gave them both the numbers of the secure satellite phones then called Jasper in England using his own to hear that Matt was finally coming to terms a little with events and that there were still repeated calls from Mihailovna pleading to speak with Ella. The bust of Mihailovna had been delivered from the casters, she had asked about it but Jasper was at a loss as to what to tell the woman and fearful of any further robbery attempts.

After collecting some much-needed food and medical supplies Fergusson had headed back to Galataria.

Chapter Forty Seven

Adam found Ella in the great room staring fixedly at the paintings. She had noticed Adam's signature on them.

"I didn't know you painted Adam."

"I'm not sure that's what you would call it. More like therapy. Karl Jung said that good and evil should not be separated that both exist in the human psyche. He called the propensity for evil the Shadow and believed that any repression was dangerous and it was better to recognize your Shadow, come to terms with it, and accept who you really are. Not all the violence in my wars was perpetrated by other people, these are an act of creation, I suppose, atonement for my acts of destruction. I think I thought that painting my soul would allow me to accept my Shadow and not see it as a separate entity. Now I just look on them as colorful daubs to brighten the walls."

"Jung may well have been right; I think I have been a danger to myself and anyone around me. I have never tried to get to know that part of me; never sifted through the silt at the bottom of my psyche, I was aware of its existence I just didn't want to acknowledge it. I've always been afraid of passion, emotional displays, that's why I think I must have channeled so much into my work the more I pushed the boundaries of my imagination the less I had to look at reality. My sculptures have been a catheter to my emotions. Too much suppression of the darker side of my soul, perhaps I should have allowed it some freedom. My family, in fact, most of my early years were surrounded by the clamor of noise and violence. I read somewhere that the abused often becomes the abuser and I was so afraid of that."

"It doesn't happen in every case and in your case perhaps you should remember and learn to be grateful for your earlier life too. perhaps memories hold the keys to all the locked doors in one's psyche bad as they may have been, fer it's what has made you who y'are. It's what has shaped your destiny made you into a fine person, a genuinely good person. I've never known ye say an unkind word about anyone. Emotions are like volcanoes they have to erupt and sometimes several small eruptions may be better than one big one."

"I tried to kill Mihailovna."

"I doubt ye meant it hen. Are ye in love with her?"

"I thought I loved her, she got under my skin, and I admired her greatly, but Gaffy wanted more than I could give, then when I tried to ___ I was crazy, I've never been jealous before but I was and something happened to me, the 'red mist' isn't that what it's called?"

"She has been calling Jazz, well calling the house for you really. You might clear the air by speaking to her. The bust you made of her has been delivered, she asked about it and Jazz is a little worried, he doesn't know what he should tell her or what to do with the sculpture."

"Tell him to have it destroyed," Ella said coldly and walked out of the room.

Chapter Forty Eight

Packer and Warrender had spent the last few days trawling through news reports and searching the internet for any information that would lead them to the whereabouts of Ella Michaels. Warrender was unhappy about the contact with Packer but could see no other way than working together to find Michaels and he wanted none of his legitimate employees involved. He had already moved the stolen sculpture to a secure place, a lock-up not far from his home but not even registered in his name.

Packer also disliked this contact but the money on offer was considerable and with what he already had stashed in a Swiss bank would probably be sufficient to allow him to retire and indulge his passion for lepidoptery. He enjoyed watching the slow fluttering of the butterflies as they died and the precision of carefully spreading and pinning them out in his display cases. He didn't like Warrender, but then he liked few people and for a moment luxuriated in the idea of pinning Warrender's ostentatious male posturing amongst his other specimens. When he found the woman and had been paid he would sever all ties with the man maybe by severing his throat he thought, he cocked his head on one side and bared his teeth in a feral smile that failed to contain any warmth.

"Well, so far we've found nothing, not a trace. Michaels company accounts, bank accounts, everything is above board and out in the open and there's no sign of any overseas properties being owned by Michaels or any of her family. Nothing at all coming from the press either, the police have put a blanket on all that and since it was one of their own that you took out, the press are complying."

"What if I go down there again, ask around, someone may know something?"

"You couldn't hang around there after hitting the reporter and the place is still crawling with police. Securicar have been busy moving any sculptures to the National Gallery along with the others from the exhibition; the police are still looking for you and would suspect any strangers in the area asking questions. I think it's down to one of my buyers now; he's upped the ante so I've told him he'll have to use the considerable resources he has. He has a vast IT empire at his fingertips I'm sure they can help to find Michaels.

Strange to think what lengths some people will go to, to own something that they can never show to anyone. I have two prospective buyers but this one is relentless in his pursuit of the rare."

Max Cauldwell had been incensed when the sculpture he had bid for at the Michaels exhibition had been snatched from his grasp and the thought that she would never make another had served to increase his determination to own the only one available. His agreement with Warrender for the stolen sculpture was two million in advance paid into a Swiss account when news of Ella Michaels death was confirmed, his representative would then oversee the authentication and removal of the sculpture and the transfer of a further eight million to the same Swiss account.

This will be both your debut and finale my lady, he thought, remembering her dismissal of him and his business at the opening evening at the Tate Gallery.

"What about Adam Fergusson? He's ex SAS lots of experience; he'll know places to hide and this firm he is using, he is the fly in the ointment."

"It's worth delving a little deeper there you're right Packer, I'll talk to my buyer; see if they can get into his files, Fergusson, as you say, is no longer active but he has connections notwithstanding the people he's using now."

Chapter Forty Nine

With police activity concentrated around Crystal and her mother's homes, no one had considered watching the Lodge which belonged to Adam Fergusson. Shutting off the alarms and gaining entry proved relatively easy. The hard drive from his desktop computer was removed and the house remained otherwise completely undisturbed.

When Hilda, Fergusson's cleaning lady arrived and let herself in with her key and the alarm didn't flash its usual red lights at her she merely presumed the battery was dead, she shrugged she didn't understand all this technical malarkey as she called it.

Wayne Harding was a geek. The world he inhabited was a virtual one, his pale spotty skin; slouched shoulders and spreading backside were perched on his usual chair in front of one of his monitors. He rarely left the womb of his grubby flat; a click of the mouse brought him a range of twenty-four-hour take away deliveries. Wayne had often worked for Cauldwell and since he had little contact with the real world he was discrete, his needs were few, Cauldwell paid well and the money was spent on more sophisticated software and the accumulated gadgetry which served to amuse him.

Foraging through deleted files, pulling out fragments and fitting them together again left Wayne in his element, and stuffing another slice of almost cold greasy pizza in his mouth he wiped his fingers on his already stained T-shirt and boxer shorts and tapped away at the keyboard.

Forty-eight hours later Cauldwell had his information and Warrender received the call he had been waiting for and rapidly contacted Packer.

"It looks like your hunch may have paid off Packer. Fergusson's financial records show ownership of a house in Cyprus, he served there for a few years so it makes sense that he may choose it. It's a place up in the hills there some 30 kilometers from Paphos and that we now know is where a Lear Jet landed at just around the right time. Get yourself out there ASAP and let me know soon as. Do whatever is necessary when you've sussed the situation out. I take it you know

where to get more men, he isn't alone as you could well imagine."

Chapter Fifty

Hiro Takana was an inveterate collector of art and antiques; he had recently paid forty million for a little known canvas attributed to Van Gogh. He sat at his magnificent seventeenth-century Hepplewhite desk overlooking the harbor in Tokyo. The dark silhouettes of the harbor walls framed the brightly lit outline of the Rainbow bridge, its' classic architectural lines ascetically pleasing, the colorful illumination of the many barges reflected in the water. The view was itself an ever-moving canvas.

On the walls behind him two large Hockneys, lots of water reflections and inviting shadows, a Klee and a Diebenkorn looking pale and exquisite. A Brancusi sat on top of a Louis XV refectory table and an Epstein bust perched on a marble plinth.

He was again reading the Times report of the attempted assassination of Ella Michaels. Takana had been present at the opening night of the exhibition at the Tate Gallery had successfully bid on one of the pieces before their withdrawal and had found Ella Michaels to be a charming woman with a formidable talent. He considered the accident potentially a great loss to the art world and her death a more final one. He recognized immediately who was behind the shooting, Warrender had been asking a high price for the stolen sculpture and whilst he had not been entirely opposed to buying stolen pieces in the past he had on further investigation taken note of the provenance of this particular sculpture. The owner he had noted had been the much-loved daughter of the sculptor, murdered during its theft, he was mindful of their short conversation on the opening night of the exhibition.

Takana was essentially an honorable man these combined facts had wrenched at his conscience for the past few days and perhaps too, he admitted to himself should the damaged limb be restored there would be more legitimate sculptures to acquire in the future. Takana pressed the buzzer of the intercom connecting him to his secretary and instructed him to put him through to New Scotland Yard in London.

Chapter Fifty One

Fergusson entered the coffee shop in search of cigarettes for Ella and Boyle. He bought several packs counting out the money for Evgenia a tiny wizened old woman dressed in the ubiquitous black of mourning and took one of the old rush seated chairs into the dappled sunshine. She brought him a demitasse of the thick viscous Cyprus coffee accompanied by a glass of cool water and placing them on a small tray she balanced the tray on yet another rickety rush seated chair. There were few tables in the coffee shop and those that existed were used for backgammon, cards, and chess.

A man joined him and they greeted each other warmly. Alfredo was 6'3" tall slim and sinewy. He was a dark nutmeg brown color from working the land in the searing hot sun, his grey hair thinning and receding off his long, weathered face which sported a large aquiline nose and a handlebar mustache which he twirled the ends of constantly. His eyes were dark heavy-lidded and brooding.

"One moment please." Alfredo stood and went to his truck, returning with a bottle of Chivas Regal, and calling to Evgenia for two glasses. Beer was available but if you wanted anything other, you brought your own.

"We speak in your tongue, better for now. You know my friend, Adam, we have few visitors here, but a few they come to taste the wine. You have visitors yourself at the moment."

Adam gave a wry smile but did not answer.

"Here we know little of culture, but my son, he have the internet now." He paused and filled their glasses. "He watches the Skye."

"Not the stars I presume." Adam drank.

"No, not the stars. You were seen." Alfredo twirled the ends of his mustache and waited until Evgenia was out of earshot.

"Not that she understands, my friend, but still, a little senile," he twirled his index finger and pointed to his head laughing, "but she is liking her nose in everything. The woman with you on the Skye, she is important to you?"

"Yes, she is important to me."

"My son he say perhaps she is important to others also, that she is a special person."

"Yes, she is."

Alfredo slowly reopened the bottle and poured two more drinks out before continuing, "These visitors that come to the winery, they do not often come to the village, sometimes, but one of them, yesterday. A man, he came to the Kafeneo, few of us speak English as you know. He did not speak Cypriot, so we did not understand his questions."

"Questions?"

"Yes, my friend, questions. This man he is not an ordinary man, he is a soldier, a maestro of death, you understand. It is in his eyes, he is very kreo. I have seen this look before."

"And where have you seen this look before, my friend."

"Why, in your eyes Adam. It is not there for many years now but once it was."

"It is still there Alfredo."

"Perhaps, beneath this belo, of the cosmos, signomi my English is not good," he gestured with his hand covering his face to signify a veil, "it is there in all of us, nai?"

"Perhaps, Alfredo. And the questions were about me?" Adam shook his head in disbelief that they could have been discovered so soon.

"Yes, this is why we did not understand him. He does not know at the moment where your spiti is. He does not leave Cyprus, he is staying at Springs of Life, you know the pension. It is ten kilometer. Springs of Life is owned by Christakis, a friend, I had to take him some bread that my wife made, you understand. He is very fond of my wife's bread. I think, or maybe it is my wife he is fond of."

"He is alone the man?" Adam interceded.

"Nai."

"He will come back."

"Nai, but now he waits." Adam looked into Alfredo's eyes, questioningly. "Christakis, he understand a little English but he does not say, the man he makes phone calls. He will not come alone."

"How many?"

"Christakis he is not sure, maybe four, and you are three, no?"

"Yes, but we will be ready now thank you, Alfredo." Fergusson wrapped a smile around his naked annoyance.

"Entaxi. Filo's moo, WE will be ready."

"Alfredo, this is not your fight, this man, as you said he is a maestro he has already killed. I'm not from here, not family and I don't want to see anyone hurt, enough people have been hurt already."

Alfredo twirled his mustache, and filled the glasses once more before answering with a smile, "True, you are not Cypriot, but you are of Galatarka and in Galatarka, we do not care for outsiders to bring trouble here. These men, my friend, do not know this land, we do, when they come, WE will be ready. Now, one more drink you sly old dog, this is a beautiful woman eh? I would like you to introduce Alfredo."

Chapter Fifty Two

Packer disliked having to use other people for a job, preferring the anonymity of working alone, no trails to follow but his own and he never left any. Sean Kelly was a course Black Irish thug well built with a bullish neck and thick dark curly hair, and Timothy Flynn his antithesis short, wiry and economic of movement, both were ex-IRA.

Ivan Veschenko a Russian living on the island had supplied guns, Russian Makarov 9 x 18mm, RG028 cartridges, enhanced penetration bullets capable of piercing any body armor, silencers, night vision goggles, and radio phones along with land registry lists and detailed ordnance survey maps of the area. To Packer's inveterate distrust of others, all three were dispensable and given this terrain easily disposable. None would be missed; no one would look for them.

All four pored over the maps reconnoitering for less obvious access to Fergusson's land, the Russian knew the island well but not these deep inland areas. The house itself had only one road leading to it, the surrounding terrain whilst not insurmountable would be difficult underfoot. Veschenko assured them though that lots of fire breaks existed that they could utilize. There appeared no road without going through the village itself but from what Packer had seen of it he had judged the bucolic inhabitants too lethargic to notice much at all.

They checked the weapons and shared out the spare magazines, synchronized their watches set the hand radios to the same frequency and packed everything into the four-wheel-drive Jeep. They were ready enough thought Packer.

Chapter Fifty Three

Alfredo was drinking his customary Cyprus coffee in the amber dusk on the tiny square fronting the coffee shop; it was seven-thirty in the evening when the Jeep bearing the red license plates of a hire car passed through the village of Galataria. He finished his coffee nodded to his son Pambolis who rose and climbing into his truck followed the car as Alfredo made a call on his mobile to Fergusson.

"They come now. Pambos is following; they are four in a Jeep, coming through the ruined Turkish village, Vretsia."

Vretsia was a small abandoned and dilapidated old Turkish village about two kilometers distant from Fergusson's property to the northeast. The distance was fairly dense woodland, tall hills and deep valleys dissected by fire breaks.

Pambos saw the Jeep make the narrow turn down into the valley heading towards Vretsia, he easily worked out their destination so allowed them to put plenty of distance between them else he would too easily be seen. The rains last winter had been the worst for seventy years and what road surfaces there were had suffered badly. Packer and his men were bounced wildly around in the vehicle as they coursed the potholes and wide fissures, like small earthquake chasms, deep ruts and a scattering of limestone rocks. The engine whined with the descent, progress was slow and it was a good half hour later as they passed through the old ruins and turned back on themselves along a wide firebreak through the thick pine and almond trees. A kilometer along they pulled into the shelter of the woods, alighted, covered the vehicle with loose branches, and proceeded on foot.

Pambos dressed in the green and brown camouflage fatigues that he wore when hunting had left his truck in Vretsia and easily covered the ground on foot. He moved stealthily through the pines a hundred yards or so behind Packer and his men. Packer wasted no energy on speech and aware that any sound would carry hand signaled for Veschenko to continue to the right of their position, bringing him close to the main driveway of the house where he would create a diversion. Flynn and Kelly were to top the ridge and drop down from above the property whilst he would go left and using the sniper's rifle pick off any opposition before moving in for the kill. It would take Veschenko a while to reach his position before creating the diversion necessary, the others would wait for his signal.

Fergusson shepherded Ella up the staircase and into the bedroom. He loaded a small-caliber lightweight Walther PPK and presented it to Ella.

"Take it."

"I've never handled a gun, and I'm right-handed, what use would it be?"

"It's just a precaution, but if anything goes wrong and one of them gets in here point it right at the center of the body and pull the trigger. If they get that close you can't miss. The gun is light with little kick from it; it'll do what it's meant to. It'll be you or them, don't hesitate."

Ella had taken the gun tentatively, Fergusson reached out and steadied the hand holding it as he levered the safety catch off.

"I'm sorry I did'ne think they'd find us here."

Ella sat on the bed staring at the pistol, her hand trembling with the weight of it and took herself into the bathroom where she climbed into the bathtub and crouched low behind its' high sides.

Alfredo had arrived by the main driveway to find Fergusson, Boyle and Styles waiting for him they shook hands and nodded to each other.

"Styles you stay by the rear of the house, Boyle you and Alfredo cover the drive, I'll go down this way to cut them off," Fergusson instructed, once again donning the mask of the consummate soldier.

Kelly and Flynn had roped themselves to two stout tree trunks which would give them purchase descending the steep incline of loose shale and rocks and now crouched down to wait. The climb had made them sweat heavily and they swatted at a funnel of angry gnats spinning in the sunlight as they sat waiting passing water from a canteen between them. Pambos sank down into the undergrowth fished the mobile from one of his capacious pockets and sent his father a text. He quietly eased the Winchester 300 hunting rifle to the ground alongside him.

Packer had found himself an elevated position within an outcrop of rocks which afforded good cover and clear sight of the target area. The Rank-Pullin had been bound in sackcloth to reduce any reflection from the sun giving away his position and setting his sights he readied himself.

Only the chattering of a few birds and the lazy buzzing of insects basking in the last of the suns rays broke the stillness, dusk, time to go thought Veschenko. He had caught a glimpse of Boyle sliding behind a low wall bordering the olive trees. He gave the requisite signal on the radio phone paused for two minutes and lobbed the flash grenade towards the house. Stark white-hot light momentarily lit up the building, blinding Boyle for a second. Veschenko rushed forward the Makarov aimed straight for Boyle when something large and heavy hit him from the side and rolled him onto his back. The sibilant swish of a blade cut the air and a glimmer of bright steel imprinted itself on Veschenko's retina, it was the last thing he saw. Blood bubbled from a deep dark slash across his throat. As Boyle moved cautiously towards the two bodies Alfredo stood and wiped the broad serrated hunting knife on his sleeve, grinned toothily and moved off to rejoin Fergusson.

Kelly and Flynn had started their descent just before the flare of light. Even with the ropes, the descent was steep and difficult with torn root clumps and loose rocks to undermine their footing they needed the sharpest of reflexes to stop them from pitching headlong down the slope. They dropped as swiftly as they could down the incline, small stones and other detritus disturbed by their motion plummeted before them when Pambos rose and followed them to the edge of the ridge, he bent and sliced through the ropes anchoring Kelly and Flynn before dropping to his knees and sighting along the barrel of the Winchester.

Kelly was caught off guard by the slackening of the guy rope and tumbled headlong down the slope, the skin of his hands was flayed by the jagged rocks as he scrabbled for purchase among them and a needle-sharp broken root tore into his thigh and embedded itself there, he landed with a crash onto the roof of the smaller house. Flynn saw nothing of Kelly's fall he was already dead, the bullet had entered the back of his skull through a small dark hole and left a gaping maw where his nose and mouth had been. Pambos crashed down the steep incline in pursuit of Kelly.

As Boyle and Alfredo moved across his vision Packer squeezed the trigger, the crack of a gunshot split the silence of the mountain air, the bullet tore through Boyl's shoulder the ensuing report like a detonation and a window of the house exploded inwards. Fergusson saw the muzzle flash and returned fire as Alfredo bent to help Boyle.

"Fucking cunt." Screamed Kelly as he righted himself just before Pambos plowed into him.

Kelly's size gave him the advantage over the slim built young man and he smashed the loose tile he held into the side of Pambos' head. Styles, pistol in hand had heard the fracas created by Boyle's fall and was edging along the side of one of the outhouses trying desperately to pinpoint him when Kelly crashed onto her like a dead weight from the roof of the wet room. She lay winded and stunned unable to move at all. How many of the fuckers is there thought Kelly through a mist of pain as he limped cautiously towards the house?

Alfredo had torn off some of his shirt and packed it into the wound in Boyle's shoulder. Boyle winced in pain as Alfredo dragged him back towards the wall and left him half sitting half propped against the stone of the house, pistol in hand. An automatic weapon stuttered as Fergusson returned fire on the sniper and was answered by the reassuring bellow of Alfredo's Winchester. Packer swore under his breath, pinned down, as a piece of rock exploded in front of him sending dust into his eyes and clouding his vision.

Ella felt the vibration rather than heard the heavy tread on the sprung slats of the staircase. Involuntarily her chest tightened and her stomach twisted into knots as she cowered shivering with fear in the bathtub. She was afraid to breathe, remembering her brother's heavy army boots climbing the stairs as she hid beneath the old iron bed. Seeing her own reflection in their shiny brightness as they paused in front of her anticipating the pain of their contact.

I know you're there Gabriella."

She heard Kelly in the bedroom, and the old memory of fear dredged itself up from the past, she felt the gun in her hand cool like the iron poker of long ago. It crossed her mind that had she had a gun then, would she have used it? As the adrenalin surged through her like a jolt of electricity Ella was galvanized into action, rose and stepped out of the tub and walked into the bedroom. She almost quailed at the monstrous sight before her; Kelly was covered in dirt and dust, his hands bloody, his face scratched and torn and a jagged piece of tree protruded from his thigh, dripping blood onto the floor. He snarled as he leaped towards her combat knife in hand.

"Cunt."

Ella raised the pistol and fired. The blast deafened her as the sound reverberated around the bedroom. Kelly slumped to the floor with a thud.

Fergusson's head snapped back at the sound of the gunshot from the house.

"Jesus! Alfredo keep me covered."

He dodged quickly back to the house, calling Ella as he rushed wild-eyed through the rooms and up the stairs. Adam almost fell over Kelly's inert form, he kicked away the knife and bent, trying to avoid kneeling in the pooling blood, to feel his pulse and confirm his death before confronting Ella's staring glazed look, the gun hanging limply by her side. Fergusson approached cautiously as though she were a wounded animal, intending to take the pistol when suddenly she struck him. The gun caught his nose and blood poured from his nostrils. Instead of stopping Ella flung the gun aside and slammed her fist into his shoulder, pummeling him, punching until her hand hurt, he made no effort to defend himself.

"Oh no, oh no," Ella wailed.

"Shhh...."

Fergusson crushed her to his chest, gentling her.

"It's okay, it's okay."

Suddenly, she wilted, sobbing, great wrenching sobs dredged from deep inside her and she shuddered and started to quake uncontrollably in his arms. He felt her bones close to the surface, delicate, so fragile now and he lifted her and laid her on the bed, stroking her hair back from her face.

Chapter Fifty Four

The firing had ceased. Pambos, his young swarthy face grinning broadly and Styles their arms around one another in support limped into the house from the back courtyard and dropped like stones onto the sofa. Alfredo came in through the front door. Fergusson was filling a syringe from the medical supplies; he tapped lightly on the cylinder, ejected a minute amount and went up the stairs.

"I need to give Ella a shot, to calm her I'm very worried about her state of mind and how it will affect the injuries she already has. I'll call Chen Lo, then we'll get Sentinel on the line. I've given Boyle a shot of morphine, some antibiotics and packed the wound but he needs a doctor and I think it best we get out of here. Our friend may be back."

"Not in the darkness I think, but soon," said Alfredo.

When he came back downstairs Fergusson had poured them all two good fingers of Laphroaig, single malt over ice and stood swirling the liquor around his glass, he swallowed and felt the alcohol rush surge through his body taking the edge of his nerves.

Packer realizing the futility of his position had slunk away into the undergrowth and gaining the Jeep had roared away. He wiped the smear of blood from his cheek where a ricocheting piece of rock had hit him and concentrated on the twists and turns of the road ahead, the lanes were narrow with steep drops on either side. Darkness in the woods was more than lack of light, it was tangible, enveloping and smothering, even with the headlights on full beam it did little to illuminate the utter blackness. Reaching the main roadway he turned upwards towards Panagia and finding a small dirt track off the road he parked, dousing the lights. He wiped the sheen of sweat from his brow and took deep breaths to still the jangle left by such a rush of adrenalin. Stretching himself across the seats he closed his eyes to concentrate better and work out his next move.

Chapter Fifty Five

Chen Lo was in his office about to call the satellite phone when Fergusson rang.

"Ah, Mr. Fergusson, you have pre-empted my call to you, but first is there a further problem?"

Adam explained what had happened and spoke to Chen Lo of his concerns regarding Ella's present state of mind.

"I too have my concerns for my patient, healing must begin in the mind. But surprising news for you and I think I can help. Ella Michaels and Jian Arts are not unknown to my government. Some years ago, Ella Michaels made a limited edition porcelain sculpture of a beautiful panda. We Chinese are very fond of our pandas and Jian Arts made a covenant with my government to give a considerable amount of money from the sale of each panda directly to the Wolong Panda Reserve in a bid to help our endangered species. This was no tax-deductible charity no simple philanthropic gesture, but had a delicate refinement allowing us Chinese to 'save face' as we say."

Jian Arts had hosted a lavish Chinese banquet at their factory which had been attended by the consul general who had been presented with one of the beautiful pandas at the signing of the covenant and Ella had personally received each New Year a card, inlaid with an exquisite hand-painted silk panel. The Chinese had responded with full press coverage both in China and Hong Kong, in the UK Prince Phillip, who was chairman of the World Wildlife Organization, for which the panda was the emblem, had been filmed with one of the sculptures sitting on a side table beside his armchair in his study and as a result the pandas had sold out.

"Ella Michaels has had a personal invitation to visit China and Wolong in particular for some time now.

It is time for Ms. Michaels to visit our giant pandas for she too has become an endangered species; also they have something else in common, yes? Pandas have opposable thumbs and for recovery, this is the major problem for our Jian. The thumb is the key to hand function and I have been working on a solution. You will accompany her I think? Ms. Michaels will need you now. We Chinese may seem distant and strange to most Westerners but we admire very much subtlety and culture and the bamboo curtain is more impenetrable than one of iron. Ms. Michaels will be safer here."

Chapter Fifty Six

At first light as the tangerine sun peeped over the surrounding hills peppered with aged sculptural olive trees their silver tips glinting, pine trees and monumental outcroppings of volcanic rock Fergusson and Alfredo had retrieved the three bodies and bundling them into the back of Alfredo's truck had driven deep into the valley to a clearing beneath the trees, then laid them out in the dirt along with their weapons

Phillipos, Alfredo's second son bore little resemblance to his father or his brother Pambos, in fact, he was the complete opposite, shorter in stature, paler skinned, he had a noble patrician head and thick trunk like arms and thighs. Phillipos had a rather stoical nature and was a common sight around the village driving one of his vehicles from a stable of tractors and diggers.

This morning he had followed Fergusson and Alfredo in the smaller of the diggers, the Hanix mini digger with its' long mechanical arm and bucket and its' orangey-yellow body the only bright splash in the dry drab colors of the summer landscape, and was now nonchalantly excavating a deep trench in the hard sun-baked soil. All traces were tossed without ceremony into the hole alongside the bodies and the digger slowly enfolded them into the earth, tamping it down tightly using the bucket.

"No one will look for them," said Alfredo as he carefully ground out the embers of his cigarette using the toe of his boot. "Fires are a bigger danger here than they proved to be."

Sentinel had moved quickly, two armored four-wheel-drive vehicles had arrived at Fergusson's house, shortly before seven-thirty in the morning and spirited the four swiftly away to a waiting Lear Jet which had flown directly to London Heathrow where Fergusson and Ella would board a flight to Singapore.

Chapter Fifty Seven

Packer retraced his journey of the previous night, this time leaving the Jeep in the ruins of Vretsia. Fucking bastard Fergusson, I'll do for you mate, he thought as he made his way through the trees and scrub close to the ridge behind the stone house. Taking a lighter from his pocket he carefully gathered dried leaves and scrub materials together into kindling and lit a fire.

Alfredo and Phillipos had made slow progress back with the small digger and as they passed through the ruined houses spotted the Jeep.

"Our friend is back my son, quickly, I think Adam will have already left but we must hurry," Alfredo spoke Cypriot to his son.

They abandoned the digger and followed Packer's tracks. Packer fed the already roaring fire with more loose branches, tentatively pulling lit ones from the inferno he tossed them down the incline towards the buildings. The fire spread rapidly in the dry atmosphere and the dark smoke spiraled above the treetops.

Alfredo noticed the smoke rising in the still air, "Bastard," he cursed, pulling his mobile out of his pocket and quickly calling the fire service, while Phillipos made several calls to local villagers, fire was something everybody here in the foothills feared.

Packer was walking backward admiring his handy work as the flames ate up the shed pine cones and needles littering the ground, sucked out the remaining air and exploded in a rush down the slope. He laughed gleefully but the laugh died in his throat as Alfredo encircled it and held the blade poised there.

"They are already gone my friend you are too late but we will let you enjoy your fire," Alfredo said quietly.

Phillipos disarmed the killer and exchanged the gun for the knife. His father held the pistol pointed to Packer's head as Phillipos took the well-honed razor-edged knife and without venom said, "Allow me," he bent to his knees and deftly sliced deeply through the Achilles' tendons at the back of both Packers' ankles effectively crippling him completely.

"Oh Christ no," screamed Packer as he was pushed forward, toppled, and momentum carried him down the incline into the blistering crackling inferno of the flames.

The villagers were blackened by soot and charcoal, sweating heavily they watched as the fire service helicopters dropped the last of their buckets of seawater from high above onto the still smoldering area. Great gouts of liquid dropped from the sky scattering and extinguishing the dying embers of the fire and along with the ash and other detritus, the charred remains of a man's body blended into the scorched smoking earth.

Chapter Fifty Eight

Their first-class flight to Singapore had been uneventful, the weariness and trauma of the past few weeks had finally exhausted them and they had slept for most of the long hours.

A representative of the People's Republic of China had met with them at Pudong International, introduced himself as Kwok Deng and then ushered them through customs and into a waiting limousine. They had explained their rapid flight and lack of luggage and in perfect English he told them that he was fully briefed and they could use the few hours available to them to replenish their wardrobes they would, of course, be accompanied at all times, he had nodded in the direction of three stone-faced men in ill-fitting suits. Fergusson was surprised, these were government agents, either Chen Lo had a good deal of pull or the Chinese really did see Ella as a friend whose safety they intended to ensure. He could see the telltale bulge of weapons beneath their jackets and nodded with approval as their eyes roamed the surrounding area, constantly alert.

Kwok had informed them there was a planned reception in Beijing shortly after their arrival and it might be pertinent to acquire something to wear that was more appropriate, he indicated their soiled travel-weary clothes and also the area surrounding Woolong he informed them was fairly cold and wet most of the time and they would need warm clothing and boots for trekking.

Fergusson and Ella visited The Super Brand Mall, with its superb variety of shops, a magnificent glass and steel structure surrounded by shops, Armani, Prada and Balenciaga among them, where they managed to acquire all that was needed for an extended stay in China along with the Louis Vuitton luggage in which to pack their purchases. Ella found the constant vigilance of the bodyguards invasive but Adam assured her that their presence was essential.

Chapter Fifty Nine

They had been ferried from Capital International airport in Beijing directly to The Lonely Planet Hotel with its pagoda rooftops and enormous beautifully carved blue dragon festooning the front. The hotel was dressed up with Liberation-era artifacts and had an established lovely Qing-dynasty courtyard, it offered a heady dose of nostalgia for a vanished age, peace and tranquility in a fast-paced world; this unusual guest house was, they were told the choice of Chen Lo.

There were five rooms on offer all decked out with paraphernalia that wouldn't look out of place in a museum: the Chairman's Residence; two author suites, named after Edgar Snow and Han Suyin and the two Concubine suites with their own private courtyards, one of which had been reserved for them. Their suite had two impressively furnished bedrooms where a liveried porter deposited their suitcases and a smiling effusive maid unpacked and put away the clothes. They found Dr. Chen Lo waiting for them with a bottle of Sir George's most wonderful Scotch whiskey not available in the hotel or any part of China he informed them pouring three large ones over ice into crystal tumblers. The bodyguards remained outside ever watchful.

While Ella soaked in a hot Badedas filled bath, allowing the steam to fog her mind along with any mirrors in the fabulous marble bathroom, Adam gave Chen Lo a full account of all that had happened, though he left out the unceremonious disposal of the bodies of the would-be assassins by the villagers. Dr. Chen Lo was worried about how these events may affect the mind and the healing process of his patient but assured Adam that tomorrow morning he would reassess the injury and that the planned stay in Wolong and the program of rehabilitation which he had set out would be beneficial.

Later they removed to the Bomb Shelter bar, also in the spirit of pastiche, where guests are pampered with wine, cigars and propaganda films from a shelter excavated by order of Vice-Chairman Lin Biao, and after a drink there Lo had arranged for them to be driven through the streets of Beijing in Jiang Qing's aging Red

Flag limousine to his favorite restaurant where he wished to regale them with the delights of his countries cuisine.

Dinner was indeed excellent and Ella marveled that the flavors and sauces were unrivaled by any that she had eaten in any western Chinese restaurant.

During the visit to the hospital, Chen Lo X-rayed the injury, removed any sutures and completed a set of tests for nerve sensitivity. The bones were knitting well and there was some response to stimulus from the nerves, he reported. The question was more what level of sensory return could be achieved in the hand itself and what finer movements would be possible in the fingers. Due to the severe tissue avulsion and nerve damage sustained in the initial injury he had not been successful in restoring the thumb and forefinger but when they returned in two months time he would be able to remove the cage and Ella would undergo a further vital operation this could be done by taking Ella's great toe and another and replacing the damaged thumb and forefinger with these.

Ella grimaced at the thought and had to explain to Chen Lo that because of an old injury to her right foot, the great toe on one foot had been severely damaged at the joint and this had had to be removed. The joint had been taken away and the toe reattached with a metal rod running through it. The toe was shorter as a consequence and although it caused her no problems it would be useless for an operation such as he was proposing since it no longer had a joint.

Lo was disappointed but of course as he explained we all have two great toes, though the great toe does affect our balance considerably and there could be some impairment of movement as a consequence of removing the second toe. He explained that there was a further option that of a transplant, providing a suitable donor could be found. With any transplant, rejection was the major problem but here in China, there had been great inroads made with experimental techniques using bone marrow transplants from the same donor. This had resulted in less rejection and less cause for the use of immunosuppressant drugs. Dr. Chen Lo had already consulted with several colleagues involved in transplant procedures and had entered Ella Michael's requirement and statistics into an international data bank to search for a donor and also placed the details with a well-known broker, in spare parts, such is the world we live in he thought.

231

Ella had been taken aback at the suggestion of using someone else's hand.

"Please," Chen Lo said, "you are the director, you are the one who sends the signal to the nerves, they are simply vehicles, messengers. As you say in English___don't kill the messenger, yes."

In the afternoon Chen Lo took them to visit the former Hutong home of Mao Zedong which lay near Bell Tower in the northern section of the Dongcheng district. The Chinese are very proud of Mao's humble origins the place was crowded with tourists and the stone building reminded Ella and Adam of Adam's rustic home in Cyprus. All three went to Houhai Lake, the gathering place of artists and intellectuals where they sat in one of the many cafes and listened as those present expressed their distress that they would not see the sculptures for real. Ella decided there and then that the whole of the exhibition would be sent on loan first to China and later to other galleries around the world.

Chapter Sixty

The Great Hall of the People glowed in its entire splendor, lit up golden against the backdrop of the starlit night sky. The central two-story edifice was raised on a stepped dais, with five mighty pillars framing each side of the massive oak double doors and reached the full height of the building to its emerald green soffits and its low peaked terracotta tiled roof, under which the emblem of China in red and gold sat. Behind the pillars, a wall of glass reflected the many lights. Two further similarly proportioned wings were set back on either side of the main building, their rows of windows dark.

The enormous ballroom was decked in almost garish green, red and gold, carvings of dragons adorned the walls and decorative banners hung from the ceiling. A sumptuous banquet had been laid out and waiters, bearing drink trays flitted agilely through the crowd of people.

Ella had expected to be greeted by an army of mud brown uniformed guests and was pleasantly surprised to find herself one of the crowd in their designer evening wear with only the occasional dress uniform in sight. Her choice had been a raw silk Balenciaga wide-legged trousers, and the long-sleeved top, one sleeve quickly and expertly tailored to hide the cage, was a mid-thigh length, slit both sides with a high mandarin collar. Kitten heeled shoes, the Chinese seemed about her height and she felt it a courtesy not to tower above them. Adam Fergusson was wearing an Armani dinner suit, white high collared dress shirt, and Gucci patent leather evening shoes, he took her by the elbow and gently steered her through the throng. She took a sidelong glance at him, his wide shoulders and military bearing and for the first time, she became aware of him as a man. Without Adam she would most probably be dead by now, he had risked his life for her and had not left her side since Crystal's murder.

The Chairman, officials and their wives and the representatives from Wolong Panda Reserve, greeted her with open enthusiasm they had waited a long time to meet her she had been told. There was no mention of the present troubles but this she put down to Chinese discretion.

Chen Lo appraised them of Ella's offer to bring the exhibition 'Prisoners' here to China on loan, their faces were wreathed in smiles, and they, in turn, presented her with a small gift to mark their esteem, the most exquisite carving of an ivory panda the small red seal on the bottom was the mark of a master carver she knew, she was completely charmed by their warmth and generosity.

Chapter Sixty One

The next morning after they had breakfasted they were given news by Kwok that a man named Warrender was under suspicion for Crystal's murder and complicity in the murder of the reporter and two other men involved in the theft at Crystal's home. The sculpture of Crystal, Matt, and their baby, however, could not be found and since this was really their only evidence Warrender was still free to move around though under constant surveillance. The hired assassin was presumed still at large and because they were to be in an area of many tourists it was considered pertinent that the bodyguard remain in place.

Ella and Adam kept their thoughts to themselves, both fully aware through a call from Alfredo that the killer in question was no longer a threat to anyone. Fergusson though remained skeptical that the danger was over, there were always men available for hire. They were once again treated to a ride in the Red Flag limousine this time to a small airfield where a military helicopter in drab khaki with the ubiquitous red star on the side awaited them. The generosity of their hosts seemed to know no bounds; the transport was to take them into the interior to Wolong for their visit to the reserve.

From the helicopter, Kwok pointed out a magnificent bridge, the Anlan Cable Bridge which crossed the Minjinag River above Yuzui which lay like a large carp in the river. Yuzui he said was a watershed to divide the river into two parts the inner and outside river. Baoping Kou sat like the neck of a bottle bringing water into the inner river from Minjiang. Once the body of the bridge was constructed of wooden blocks and the handrails were made of bamboo but that had been when it was first constructed way back before the Song Dynasty but now they had been replaced with steel and reinforced concrete for the safety of the visitors and the bridge was completely full of them and resembled a rainbow hanging over the river as the tourists stared out at the entire layout of the Dujiangyan system and its wonderful scenery.

The Wolong Panda Reserve was to the east of Mt. Qionglai a three-hour drive from Chengdu but for Ella and Adam just a mere forty-five minutes in the helicopter. The Sichuan Giant Panda Sanctuaries are located in the southwest Sichuan province of China and are home to more than thirty percent of the world's highly endangered Giant Pandas. The area covers some 9245 square kilometers and has seven nature reserves and nine scenic parks located in the Qionglai and Jiajin Mountains. The sanctuaries are a refuge to other endangered species also such as the red panda, the snow leopard, and the clouded leopard. Apart from tropical rainforests it is botanically one of the richest sites, of the world with thousands of species of flora and looking down upon it, it resembled the paleo-tropical forests of long ago.

Chapter Sixty Two

When they left the helicopter they traveled on a bicycle driven rickshaw, quaint thought Ella until she realized the passage through the narrow cobbled streets their steepness lessened only by stone steps every two yards to make progress easier, would be impassable by car. Small stone bridges traversed the streets high above them and as the houses leaned in towards each other they seemed all that kept them from crashing together.

They passed through ornate wooden gates into a large walled courtyard where ducks and geese lay around a decorative Lilly strewn pond golden carp slid like ghosts beneath its deep green depths. Three carved stone steps led to a large pagoda-shaped house, its white stucco stained grey in places by rain. Intricately designed grey stone pillars flanked the large green doors. The pillars were an artifice of the architect they held nothing aloft and celadon lion dogs stood on guard either side of the doorway.

Inside the spacious rooms, stone floors were covered in large beautifully patterned turquoise silk rugs, the sofas and chairs were a heavy dense wood with comfortable down silk-covered cushions heavily embroidered with dragons and flowers and black and gold lacquered cabinets and a desk sat against the walls of the room.

A small wizened man, grey hair in a long pigtail and with a straggly goatee, and two giggling bowing girls presented themselves. The man wore grey baggy trousers, a tunic with a mandarin collar and slit sides and a quilted gilet for warmth. His eyes had a pale washed-out look with deep laughter lines in the corners. He passed a letter to Adam Fergusson.

Honourable Friend Adam Fergusson

There is in our excellent Ms. Michaels much more to heal than the injured arm, I sense when I look into her eyes that she has been weeping forever. It is time to dry the tears, to heal much deeper scars and more painful wounds than her injured arm.

Here she will be called Jian a necessary subterfuge, to safeguard you understand against the discovery of her identity but also most appropriate.

Chang Nai-chou is not only an excellent cook but is a most renowned sensei and exponent of Taijiquan, he is an old friend, and it will be his place to help our Jian to refocus her qi.

I rely on you Adam Fergusson, most honourable friend to see that this is done and look forward to our next meeting.

Your friend

Dr. Chen Lo

Kwok and their two bodyguards had for once made themselves scarce they were to stay in one of the smaller houses inside the walled enclosure. The giggling girls helped with the unpacking and ran a hot bath for Ella. Hot towels awaited her, silk baggy trousers and the most beautiful black kimono heavily embroidered with cherry blossoms had been laid out for her to wear. Chang made a wonderful dinner served by the effervescent ladies who turned out to be SunYin and Sun Huey. Fergusson eyed them warily since most of their tittering and chattering seemed to be about him though whatever amused them both he and Ella remained in the dark about. Kwok who had joined them for dinner was pleased that Ella had chosen to wear the kimono and explained that kimonos were often considered great works of art.

He went on to say that the kimono has another name, gofuku (literally

"clothes of Wu"), the earliest kimonos were heavily influenced by

traditional Han Chinese clothing, known today as hanfu or kanfuku

in Japanese. Ella looked to Adam and had to suppress the laugh that

was threatening to bubble out.

"I can understand why Westerners call it a kimono," said Ella

looking down at her bowl.

The steaming bath and dinner had left Ella feeling content, but

weary with the travel and she and Adam lounged on the sofas along

with one another and finally able to relax and talk over a few drinks,

vodka and tonic for Ella and Scotch for Adam. He explained the letter

from Lo Chen and Ella told him all about the Jian panda, laughing at

Lo Chen's proposed change of name for her and now that Kwok had

left them the Chinese and Japanese words for the kimono.

Chapter Sixty Three

The next morning was to set a precedent for the remainder of their stay as to a background of the purple grape-like blooms of the Jacaranda, Wisteria, and the bright vivid hues of Bougainvillea and the heady scents of Orange Blossom Chang Nai-chou began to explain the components of Taijiquan.

The discipline of internal training included stance training Zhan Zhuang stretching and strengthening of muscles, which can contain quite demanding coordination from posture to posture and focus on the practice of such elements as awareness of the spirit, mind, qi (breath, or energy flow) and the use of relaxed leverage rather than unrefined muscular tension. One of the prominent characteristics of the style is that the forms are generally performed at a slow pace this is to improve coordination and balance by increasing the workload and to require the student to pay minute attention to their whole body and its weight as they perform each technique. All this Chang explained in his quiet modulated voice as he proceeded to guide Ella through the movements. Laughter found its way back into Ella's life as she struggled to hold some of the more difficult poses and seemed to spend quite some time falling onto her backside leaving it black and blue for the first few weeks.

During one session Ella shook her head violently in irritation trying to resist the urge to scratch at her injured arm and tear open the skin; she had lost her concentration yet again because of it and cursed the arm and hand almost wishing for a moment that she had lost it.

Chang Nai-chou laughed gently and spoke, "Jian, legend tells of a man bitten by a spider as a child, the bite healed but the spot always itched, later in battle the man lost the arm to a Samurai sword, but the arm always itched in the same place on the arm that was no longer there.

It was because it is said that the spider's bite had not finished its life, like stars that go on shining long after they are dead. The feeling has not run its course the itching means there is still life it is not finished yet. Now focus, gather your thoughts."

The pain of grief lessened with each day spent in this strange faraway place.

Chapter Sixty Four

Max Cauldwell was a ruthless man, a man who hated to lose, whatever the game. He desired the Michaels sculpture with a passion but he wanted it to be the only one in private possession, such was his nature. So far Michaels had disappeared, totally evaporated and with all his resources he could find no information at all.

Warrender was a fool and Cauldwell had strung him out, the man was now desperate, already under suspicion and running scared. Cauldwell could not be seen to have any connection with the man and contact was kept to a minimum using secure satellite phones just in case Warrender's normal phone lines were bugged. The sculpture would be his but not for the previous price offered and once in his possession he would wait until Michaels surfaced again and she would he was sure of that. But first, there was Warrender to deal with.

Cauldwell was right Warrender was afraid; the sculpture was well hidden for the moment but he knew that his every move was watched and his paranoia was escalating. A new deal was on the table, a million cash and a new identity, he was tempted to just sit it out forget the bloody sculpture and carry on with his life, the police had no evidence without it. He was though afraid of Cauldwell, the man was relentless and once in possession, he would certainly kill Michaels if she ever showed up, as for him he feared that Cauldwell would tie up any loose ends and that included himself. For the moment being watched by the police was like having private protection but for how long would it last? He feared also that Caldwell's resources might be able to track down the location of the lock-up and steal the sculpture from him or even try to force the information as to the whereabouts of the sculpture from him without paying for it, he needed a bargaining point which would keep him alive long enough to transfer money electronically and get far enough away at the same time.

Warrender made a call on an unregistered mobile he thought perhaps some kind of insurance would be a wise move.

A few hours later he answered the same mobile, "Is the device in place?"

"Yes, the sensors will detect touch and certainly any attempt to move the crate, a little like a car alarm; you have two minutes to punch in the code as requested."

"Fine, the money will be transferred to your account."

Pete Robinson flipped the mobile closed. He had known Warrender for some years, worked for him before, mainly on burglaries, Robinson was an explosives expert and learned his trade in the army before getting a dishonorable discharge. The money was good though and it was not for him to question why Warrender might feel the need to blow up a packing crate in the old lock-up beneath the railway arches.

Chapter Sixty Five

Ella had received a terrific reception at the Panda reserve and had been heartened to see one of her porcelain pandas in a specially made glass case; a brass plaque attributed it to her and beneath it was written how much money had been raised. It took pride of place in the showroom area where souvenirs could be bought by the many tourists and she was treated with the deference of visiting royalty.

Most of her and Adam's afternoons were spent at the reserve, helping in the breeding program, feeding and playing with the pandas and occasionally trekking out in the dense forest, their guide waving his radio tracking device in the air as they searched for tagged pandas to check on them.

Working with Cheng on the Taijiquan techniques, meditation and trekking through the forests looking for pandas had made Ella sturdier of mind and body, her muscles were well-toned and her mind focused, she had even begun to laugh again, playing with young pandas was a wonderful experience like your favorite toy coming to life. The guards were as shadows, ever-present, but not noticed on a conscious level, they worked always to maintain space around the couple and whilst she and Adam had tried to avoid much contact with the tourists it was inevitable that some took place.

There are over 4,000 different species recorded in the reserve. Wolong National Nature Reserve houses more than 150 highly endangered giant pandas. The reserve is also home to many other endangered species including red pandas, golden monkeys, white-lipped deer, and many precious plants. Wildlife observation spots opened in the reserve attract explorers, tourists, animal-lovers as well as scientists. Many tourists take photos of themselves with the tiny mouse-like babies, and occasionally wild pandas may show up in the Reserve. Wolong gets up to 100,000 visitors every year,

Unfortunately, research shows that the current rate of destruction of the environment is higher after the reserve's creation than it was before. Using NASA's satellite images and records of population, research teams have concluded that due to tourism and the increase in the local population, the reserve is facing an unprecedented threat.

Tourists don't think they have an impact on the panda habitat, but indirectly each visitor has some. We don't see ourselves as a destructive force, but we are.

"Jeez I wish I was as popular with the guys as she is, they are like bees round a honey pot."

"Are you crazy? Those guys are packing, didn't you notice the telltale bulges and most of them never say anything. I'm guessing she is quite important somehow and here the guides even treat her differently to the rest of us."

"What'd you mean like bodyguards? Well, who the hell is she?"

"I couldn't help overhearing but I think I know who she is," interrupted another tourist, a middle-aged English man traveling alone.

"Yeah, well I think she's English, like you."

"I recognize her from the news a little way back, she's Ella Michaels, I think the panda in the shop has something to do with her, I think she raised quite a bit of money for this place. She was injured in some car crash but someone tried to kill her and a reporter got shot instead, her daughter was murdered too, all over some sculptures that were stolen, I think, and she was involved with that tennis player, Mihailovna."

"Wow, that's who it is, so she's gay anyway?"

"Now that I don't know."

"Well, I managed to get a bit of film on my mobile when no one was looking, can't wait to put it on YouTube now."

Chapter Sixty Six

Cauldwell could not believe what he was seeing; weeks of waiting and searching had finally come down to this scrappy piece of amateur film on YouTube picked up by accident by one of his men's wives, she just happened to be crazy about pandas. The shot lasted a mere three minutes and the quality was mediocre but there could be little doubt when he focused on the cage protecting the injured arm that this was Ella Michaels. He would though make certain.

China, the bamboo curtain, not the easiest place to access he thought. In the past he had had some dealing with certain Tongs, he also had an interest in Chinese artifacts and had procured the odd rare find through them.

Operating in China could, they told him prove exceedingly difficult, and exceedingly expensive, but they could have a man there within forty-eight hours they promised. Cauldwell considered his options, he did not have the sculpture yet, but police surveillance on

Warrender had slackened a little recently most probably caused by budget limitations, he decided to await confirmation from the Tong's man, moving too soon would only alert them, and he could lose them again.

The men watching Warrender were ordered to stay alert and report on his habits in general, he needed Warrender alone to secure the whereabouts of the statue and then wipe away anything and anybody leading to himself.

Chapter Sixty Seven

"Fulong Temple is said to be the place where Li Bing subjugated the evil dragon during the construction process of Dujiangyan. The stone statue of Li Bing carved in the Eastern Han Dynasty (25-220) displayed here in the front courtyard; is the earliest sculptured stone statue found in China." Kwok, their walking encyclopedia informed Ella and Adam, "In the back courtyard of the temple, you can see the working principles of Dujiangyan replicated in an electric model of the irrigation system."

Over drinks Adam had asked Ella about the possibility of her sculpting in stone or wood and Ella had confessed that it was not something she had ever tried, the feel of the supple clay had always been what inspired her work and Kwok who occasionally joined them in the evening had suggested this trip to the Fulong Temple to see the famous old stone statue.

As they moved closer to the stone effigy a short smiling Chinese tourist had made inroads through the crowd to take a photograph, Ella moved aside to give him a better view of the stone but he had laughed saying, "Please to stay, it is a good contrast."

One of the guards had tried to move him on but when the tourist protested, they had patted him down and finding no concealed weapons had finally shrugged and turned away. He took a couple of snaps with his mobile then backed off bowing and thanking Ella effusively.

In a quiet corner of the temple courtyard, it took him mere moments to send the photos through the ether to his bosses and for them to relay it to Cauldwell.

Adam was checking his email later when a small news item with the accompanying YouTube film flashed across the top of the Yahoo Home Page. "Shite!" he shouted.

"What?" laughed Ella.

"Look at this."

"Oh God, what should we do, do you think it matters now?"

"I don't want to take that chance___ Kwok," he called. "I think we had better just step up security, for now, I'll talk to Chen Lo."

Chen Lo was not particularly distressed at the news, "Once again you have pre-empted my own call, and I think I have some very good news for my Jian. Leave tomorrow, I can be available and I think we can safely bring forward the surgery, I will arrange things from here."

The Tong's man reported that there was too much activity; the target looked to be preparing to move. He was instructed to stay as close to them as possible they would have someone on station watching in Beijing.

"We will not lose her, this is maybe more auspicious, too many tourists in Wolong." Cauldwell was told.

The press had picked up on the YouTube film and there had been a few other reported sightings since. Cauldwell banged his fist down hard onto his desk in his offices in New York, making pens and papers bounce, he could hold off for now, his eyes flashed with anger as he ordered Warrender's watchers to stand down for the time being.

Chapter Sixty Eight

Mihailovna emerged from the gymnasium in the Georgian villa she had bought on Eastbourne's Esplanade; her skin was slick with the sheen of sweat, her hair plastered to her skull after the heavy workout.

"You need to read this." Anna held the tabloid paper out to Gaffy showing her the headline.

MIHAILOVNA SEDUCED ME

JANA DJOCHEVNIC TELLS ALL

The beautiful Jana Djochevnic seventeen-year-old, shining new star of the tennis world tells our reporter how lesbian Mihailovna seduced her with gifts and promises to become her coach and take her to the heights of world tennis. The seventeen-year-old virgin was lured to Mihailovna's bedroom at the large detached rented villa on Canizaro Road in Wimbledon Village home of the wealthy

Wimbledon set and the area where most visiting world players stay during the famous tournament.

On the evening of the Ladies final at Wimbledon where young Jana had narrowly lost to Mihailovna the stars of the tennis world were partying after the tournament and naïve young Jana had been specifically invited by Mihailovna.

Renata Djochevnic was aware of the tennis star's interest in her daughter Jana's mother had warned her young daughter to stay away from Mihailovna who she had heard rumors about, rumors that Mihailovna was something of a sexual predator.

When the party was in full swing Mihailovna asked the young Jana to fetch her sweater from the bedroom for her but as she was looking for the said sweater Mihailovna entered the bedroom and started kissing and fondling the girl. Jana tells us how Mihailovna was forcing her down onto the bed, practically raping her when Michaels burst into the room. Ella Michaels, the famous sculptor, who had arrived at the party following a triumphant first exhibition at the Tate Gallery, caught Mihailovna in the act. Jana tells us that Michaels pulled Mihailovna off her and struck her before rushing out of the house where she fell victim to a serious accident which caused the loss of her hand. Mihailovna who has retired from world tennis after a glowing career has taken up residence here in England in Eastbourne, she was unavailable for comment. Ella Michaels has been in hiding since shortly after that night. Michaels' daughter was killed during a robbery at her home when one of Ella Michaels' sculptures was stolen is believed to be in fear of her life after an assassination attempt at the funeral of her daughter when our own reporter Sam Willis was sadly gunned down by mistake.

Michaels has recently been spotted in China.

"Hmm, jeez, I can't believe they have printed this."

"Well, I suppose technically they are merely reporting what the little slut has told them."

"The only person I care about seeing this isn't around to read it anyway, what do I care?" She tossed the paper into the bin.

"Gaffy, I'm sure they have papers or the internet wherever she is."

"She won't believe it, I'm sure she won't."

"Don't be too sure, anyway it isn't going to be good, folks may not want you coaching their kids after reading this crap and some may well pull out if they are crazy enough to believe it."

Chapter Sixty Nine

Anna had been right, of course, the last twenty-four hours had seen nothing but cancellations; the majority of parents of young girls were not prepared to risk their precious little darlings to a raging lesbian. The papers were full of follow up stories and sightings of Ella Michaels, who was apparently in China. Gaffy was sitting staring at the laptop screen, watching the small film on YouTube over and over again. It was Ella of course, fuzzy but Gaffy could see the ugly metal brace covering the hand and arm.

"Don't take it so hard Gaffy, it'll be a one day wonder tomorrow it will be some other poor bastards turn. You read the article, it's just crap, no one who knows you will believe a word, and everyone will know it's just that God awful mother of Jana's. It's well known on the circuit that she would do anything for money; she needs it to find a good coach since they fired the other one and you are obviously not taking her on, and for heaven's sake stop watching that piece of film. If she is in China, she is a long way from where we are right now."

"I suppose you're right, you usually are," answered Gaffy with a small smile that developed into a sigh.

"Come on Gaffy, I'm going stir crazy here, let's go paint Brighton red, or should I say pink. What we need are a couple of great chicks, just right for the plucking. At least I do, so get some glad rags on and let's hit the road."

Maiti's was a great cocktail bar on Baker Street, in the heart of busy cosmopolitan Brighton with its bright lights, bars, and bistros lively with customers spilling out onto the pavements and buzzing with conversation and snatches of music. At six pounds a throw for any cocktail you could name, and a barman who could throw them standing in front of the high bar against a backdrop of every drink, or mixer you could think of, Maiti's was full, populated with middle-class professional gays sitting in tight couples or larger groups for whom the night was young. The walls were lined with oil paintings by local artists providing talking points and the ambiance as usual was positively glowing in the general hubbub.

Anna and Gaffy ordered two Margaritas, the barman recognized Gaffy and felt assured of a good tip, he juggled the limes and lemons in the air finally letting them fall into the electric juicer, took two cocktail glasses from the freezer, the warm air misted them immediately, tossed the Tequila and the Triple Sec in the air, pirouetted and poured them into the cocktail shaker along with the crushed ice and the juice, salted the rims of the glasses with sea salt and popped them on the bar, he shook his little ass, tossing the gleaming silver shaker and when he was satisfied the girls were happy poured them into the glasses showing his gleaming white teeth in a beaming smile.

"There you go, girls."

He had managed to raise a smile out of Gaffy, earning him his generous tip. The women took the drinks and found a quiet seat in a corner.

For Joy and Ao, who lived in Hove, Maiti's was a regular drinking haunt. Joy had smoked a couple of spliffs before going out and had downed the best part of a bottle of Rioja, her eyes were bleary with cannabis and alcohol, she had been incensed by the newspaper article about Jana Djochevnic and the following reports that Ella her been found, when she spotted Mihailovna, the perfect target for her pent up outrage.

"I don't fucking believe it," she slurred to Ao, "Look what the cat dragged in."

She staggered as she stood and snorted down her nose as Ao tried to hold her back.

"Let it go Joy."

Joy shook her head, raised a hand and wagged her forefinger in front of Ao, "No." She lurched across the crowded room to confront Mihailovna.

"You know who this is____you know? This is the fucking great Mihailovna, hmm___ the greatest tennis player in the world, and the biggest pile of shit I've ever met," she announced to the room.

Barb the owner of Maiti's stood a worried frown on her face. "Joy? What's going on? Ao?"

"You know her?"

"Well I've seen her here a couple of times," said Barb.

"Hmm, this is the great Mihailovna, the two-timing fucking cow who nearly got my lovely Elly killed. Lost her fucking arm___ running away, hiding____ because of her, this bitch here."

Turning to Mihailovna Barb spat out, "I should have recognized you, you are not welcome here, I know Ella Michaels, and you Joy, leave it now, Ao take her home, she's had enough eh."

"Come on Joy."

Joy shrugged them off leaning forward her fists resting on the table Anna and Gaffy were sitting at. Anna's eyes darted around the room full of people who had all turned to watch and listen, the mood had turned ugly.

"What you still doing here, hey____you bitch, what you still doing here in England?"

"Look, Joy, I___I'm sorry, look I love Ella, I___I'm waiting___"

"Waiting?" Joy laughed a dry bitter sound. "Waiting are you, waiting for Elly, do you really think she would ever want to see you again. Her fucking daughter is dead because of you, her beautiful daughter___you ruined her life, she can't come here, can't come home. I knew she was coming to you that night, she told me, she was happy___I encouraged her___you with your words of love, insinuating yourself into her life, she believed you, I believed you, you fucking slut.

"It wasn't like that___ Joy please___"

"Gaffy come on, you need to leave."

"That's right run away, my Elly she's had to run away, why shouldn't you run. Bastard, I aught to kill you for what you've done. Look at you, out on the pull, trawling while Ella hides away frightened, grieving." Her face was wet with tears now; great heaving sobs shook her shoulders.

"Let's go Joy, and you Gaffy, if I were you I wouldn't come round here again." Ao fought to get Joy to leave, steered her away but at the last moment she spun glass in hand and threw the contents full into Gaffy's face, launching herself, fists flailing. She caught Gaffy a glancing, stinging blow on the temple before Barb forced her considerable bulk between them.

"Okay, that's enough now, Joy leave it be, and you Mihailovna, don't come back."

Anna was shocked by the angry stares and more than a little frightened but Gaffy's eyes were full of sadness as she turned resignedly and left.

Ao sat Joy down with another drink, excused herself and slipped out of the clamour of Maiti's. She found Gaffy and Anna in the dark street, trying to call a taxi. Gaffy was wary as Ao approached.

"It's okay Gaffy, I came to apologize for Joy," she lightly touched the small swelling on the side of Gaffy's face.

"No apology please, she___she loved Ella."

"Yes I know, I guess I've always known only now it's all she talks about, Ella and the accident, she's depressed all the time. I think things have run their course with us besides I er, I want___" Ao let the sentence trail away as she placed her luscious pink-brown lips to the wound, and whispered, "call me." She slid a card into the pocket of Gaffy's shirt.

Chapter Seventy

Judith Charles at fifty years of age was too young in this day and age to be called a spinster simply because she was unmarried but in fact, the word described her very well. She was 5'8" tall and very spare with mousy hair turning grey that she wore twisted into a plait and held up with a plain plastic comb. Her features were gaunt, her nose pointed and her teeth a little prominent, at school she had been called Mouse by her friends which were never many and Ratty by those who disliked her which were rather more. Judith was a vegan, didn't smoke and had never touched alcohol. She played the piano quite well but with little exception and had taught music at King Edwards Grammar School in Louth Lincolnshire for the past twenty-five years.

Nothing very remarkable had ever happened to Judith, she had lived an exemplary life, was a good Christian, a regular church attendant at St. James' Louth where apart from her attendance at services she was a member of the choir and enjoyed their many concert venues. Twice a year she visited London, once for the summer exhibition at the National Gallery which she constantly promised herself she would submit one of her paintings to but never found the confidence and the other for anything of interest at the Tate Gallery and usually on each visit she took in a show, preferably a musical, she was partial to Andrew Lloyd Weber's work, her favorite being Cats which she had seen four times to date.

As a student at Loughborough, she had studied music and art and still whiled away many an hour painting her small watercolor landscapes of the Lincolnshire Wolds. The only claim Judith had to any fame had been that she had always had beautiful hands, and had for a few years earned a little extra money as a hand model for a well-known moisturizer and occasionally a nail varnish company.

Being single had ceased to worry Judith, she would have liked to have been married and had a family but when both her parents had become infirm had elected instead to remain at home with them and see to their care. Her mother had died ten years ago of cancer and her father, an eminent geologist with congenital heart failure, having undergone a heart transplant survived for a further five years. Her only sister Jean was married with two children and her nephew and niece had become surrogate offspring who she enjoyed indulging occasionally for a day out with the advantage of being able to give them back to their parents when the day was over. It was in fact where she was heading on that busy Saturday morning to collect the children and take them to The Deep; an outstanding new aquarium in Hull which she considered would be not only enjoyable but also educational.

Judith's car had a punctured tire a couple of weeks earlier and she had replaced it with the rather worn spare. She had been somewhat distracted lately and rather busier than usual and quite out of character had forgotten to change the tires back. As she traveled in her late father's well preserved Morris Minor down the busy A16 to Grimsby the worn tire blew out, the road was wet and slick, Judith fought hard for some three hundred yards. Twelve long seconds that felt like twelve long hours, she grasped hard at the steering wheel her hands claw-like and white with strain, spun it hard and tried to stop the skid but she overcorrected in her panic and steered herself directly into the path of an oncoming Eddy Stoppard truck. The Morris rolled over and over for some three hundred yards, careering off another vehicle traveling in the same direction as her and finally came to rest upside down in one of the deep dikes running on either side of the road. The car quickly filled with water and by the time the ambulance men had removed Judith's sodden body there was little pulse, she was rushed to Grimsby hospital where the medical staff in attendance failed to revive her.

"I am very sorry for your loss Mrs. Carter, your sister is on a life support machine which is breathing for her, but there is no brain activity whatsoever, she is though a card-carrying donor and we would like____."

"Our father had a heart transplant some years ago, that would be why, its what she would do, what she would want, for Judith it would mean something good would come out of such a senseless death."

"Apart from the card etcetera, we still like to confirm with relatives. We have to act rather quickly in these circumstances and we have prospective recipients for the organs of course."

"That's fine, my sister__ my sister led a good life, I'm sure someone will benefit."

"We do have another prospective recipient, however, it is a rather sensitive area, it is not exactly an organ, it is for one of Miss Charles's hands." "What! Oh no! No. That's grotesque."

Chapter Seventy One

Francis Rossi was a slick operator; he referred to himself as The Broker. His thousand dollars suits were immaculately tailored, his silk ties subdued, after all, he had to deal with the bereaved and it wouldn't do to come across like some ambulance chaser. Spare part surgery was a growing industry to him, his clients were politicians, champions of industry even royalty, all of them desperate to prolong their lives to preserve what they saw as their legacy to the rest of the human race, lives they often thought of as indispensable to the rest of the world at large, whether the world at large agreed or not, they did not wish to linger on any waiting lists and Francis Rossi had made it his business to see that they did not.

He had not dealt with Chen Lo in a professional capacity before, but Rossi's reputation was known to many of Chen Lo's colleagues who had recommended Rossi and Frank Rossi's interest had been piqued when he had heard what Chen Lo was seeking. The Ella

Michaels story interested him, he had an affection for fine art that he attributed to his Italian heritage and Ella Michaels' legacy was one legacy he felt deserved to be preserved.

"Mr. and Mrs. Carter, my deepest sympathy, I understand your sister is donating her organs, a most estimable act."

"It's what Judith would have wanted; our father had a transplant, heart, some years ago, I'm sure that was what Judith had in her mind when she made the commitment, Ron, you agree?"

"Yes, of course, my dear." Ron Carter agreed with his wife, as he usually did.

"An estimable act, as I said. Tell me about your sister Mrs. Carter."

"About Judith, well what can I say really, Judith was a good woman, a good person, a kind, gentle, woman. She lived a very quiet life really. She played the piano, not to concert standards maybe but very well nevertheless; at least we always enjoyed it." She reached a hand out to her husband for confirmation. "She loved her musicals often went to London for them, she painted watercolors, we have several of them, quite delightful, at least we think so. Her life wasn't very eventful I suppose, except for the adverts. She was very proud of that, she had lovely hands, used to do ads for hand cream and nail polish. They were lovely, weren't they Ron, her hands?"

"Yes dear, quite lovely."

"That's what's so awful about this___ asking for one of her hands. Judith wouldn't like that, she was really proud of them, used to go to a professional manicurist even a bit extravagant that in my opinion, but she was so proud of them, her hands. It's just unthinkable."

Francis Rossi reached out and took Mrs. Carter's hands in his own, the better to empathize with her completely. "Jean, may I call you Jean?" he asked doing it anyway. "My clients as a whole are not without resources should we say, there could be substantial benefits involved. Of course, no one wants to think of benefiting from a loved one's loss but you have children I presume, their education__"

"Oh dear no, we wouldn't want to benefit at all. We loved Judith." She seemed to want to convince herself more than Rossi at this moment.

"Mrs. Carter let me be frank with you. In these circumstances, recipients of donors are normally kept anonymous, for everyone's benefit of course. But here, the request is somewhat unusual I grant you. The recipient is an absolute match and I could tell you that I am certain that your sister would approve, the recipient is a very famous artist."

There was a pause before Jean Carter had her sudden epiphany, her eyes widened and her mouth dropped open, she grasped her husband's hand. "Oh goodness, you mean her, Ella Michaels, but, but she is from here, from Lincolnshire why she only lives a few miles away. Oh my goodness. She never occurred to me but I suppose she should have of course. Judith went you know, went to the exhibition, why she couldn't stop talking about it, how wonderful the sculptures were. Oh dear Ron, what do you think?"

"Well my dear, that decision would be up to you, but I can't help thinking that Judith might have quite liked the idea, that she would be a part, so to speak, of a famous artist, um___ especially one that she approved of." For once Ron Carter had an opinion plus the thought of his children's further education being without loans was beginning to work its way through his consciousness.

"Oh my, they tried to kill her, here at the crematorium, it must have been terrible in the midst of all that grief and that poor man the reporter. Oh my, Ron may be right, perhaps Judith is looking down on us___ would want this."

Francis Rossi was very good at reading people; he had seen the slight glimmer of avarice in Ron Carter and established in his mind that the sale was already made now they merely needed to haggle over the price.

Chapter Seventy Two

"I invited Sir George to fly in to help; we do not always travel fastest when we travel alone."

Chen Lo and Sir George were poring over the x-rays.

"As you are aware my Jian you have already been undergoing a series of immunosuppressant drugs unfortunately these drugs given to transplant patients greatly lower the body's immune system this puts transplant patients at a much greater risk of cancer, infections, and other disorders and normally you would be required to take them for the rest of your life and to be extra vigilant to guard against infection of any kind. You must be more careful with your general health in the future but we will also be using experimental techniques using bone marrow transplants from the same donor. This has a way of almost fooling the body into thinking that the transplanted organ or limb is a part of the recipient's body and has greatly reduced the instances of rejection and should hopefully mean that we can reduce the amount of such debilitating drugs. However, the blood tests and crossmatch is perfect, we think that we have the perfect donor and we have great hope for success,

The hand transplant procedure is generally thought to be technically easier than a replant because the transplanted tissues have not been damaged due to traumatic injury. The procedure involves the transplantation of bone, muscle, tendon, joint, nerves and arteries all of these we will be undergoing during the operation. There has been a temptation to render limb transplants simply unethical and selfish on the parts of both surgeon and recipient. After all, lives are not at risk with the loss of a limb as they are when organ transplants are necessary; in your circumstances, this transplant is necessary not only to your quality of life but for a greater purpose."

Ella awoke groggy from the ten hours of surgery but relieved and heartened to find the steel cage had finally been removed though the new sutures still looked ugly and the area surrounding the thumb and forefinger was discoloured and swollen and since the thumb and finger bones there had been pinned the hand should not be overly used at present, certainly nothing strenuous and although for the moment it still did not feel like her hand later the scars would fade somewhat she was told. The fine bones of the hand itself had knitted together well and some sensation had returned. Chen Lo had explained that two of the fingers had little nerve restoration, these two fingers could be replaced with toes though since their general function was less important to the use of the hand for cosmetic purposes they could remain as they were, but if left in place Ella must be aware that they were unlikely to feel the danger of heat etcetera. For the rest of the hand, though the arm was two inches shorter now, the transplant had been successful and the prognosis was good, but it would be a long way to full recovery. Ella must continue with an arduous exercise regime and a course of drugs for some time.

Francis Rossi had personally traveled to China with the hand and the bone marrow in a chill container full of Ringer's lactate or saline solution. He was feeling a rare moment of sentimentality; this job was a little insurance for when he arrived at those pearly gates, one of his few altruistic gestures, redemption for an otherwise selfish life. He wanted to meet Ella Michaels, his life was peppered with people whose motives were questionable, and for once he wanted to meet with someone truly extraordinary.

He sat with Adam Fergusson, crossed-legged on a cushion, drinking green tea from tiny exquisite porcelain cups, while they waited for the operation on Ella Michaels to be over. His sharp Armani suit was becoming crumpled and was in direct contrast to Adam's, loose-fitted linen pants and shirt. He was uncomfortable and said so.

"This is killing me man, how about we sit on real chairs, and I could use a couple of bourbons over ice."

"I only have Scotch, but if that's okay, I'll join you."

They took their whiskey over to the sofas with their downy silk cushions. "Better?" asked Adam.

"Yeah, sure."

"What did we have to pay in the end?"

"100,000 pounds is all, I figured 50,000 each for the kid's college funds, and I didn't factor myself into the equation."

"That was good of you. What were they like, what was she like the donor?"

"Unremarkable really apart from the hands, they were beautiful. She was I think a good woman, religious. She did a bit of painting, watercolors, they showed them to me, well the sister did.

No worse than my own, I do a bit myself, find it relaxing, you?"

"Yes, for my sins, I don't rate them, Ella seems to quite like them. What was she like, the sister?"

"I think she felt she loved her sister, or at least tried to. She didn't want to play ball at first, thought it was bizarre but I convinced her that her sister would be looking down from heaven feeling a part, forgive the pun, a part at least of a great artist, someone she had admired. He was the cruncher, when I mentioned money, I could see it in his eyes, always can, it's like calling a woman a whore and she protests she's not, so you ask her if you gave her a $1,000,000 would she fuck you and she considers it. You've already established what she is, you're just haggling the price. He convinced the sister it would be what Judith wanted."

Adam laughed, "I think that was something Winston Churchill was supposed to have said to Lady Astor one time. It's a strange business your in Rossi."

"Yeah, but I found my niche market, this is a growing trade."

Chapter Seventy Three

They returned to the area of Houhai Lake where they were to stay in a small house with an adjoining art studio, in the area where the artists gathered they were taken to the workshop of an esteemed sculptor. The shelves were crammed with an orgy of delicate pieces of ivory and jade that were superbly executed and a fine scent of jasmine filled the air. The artist bowed low to Ella, gave a shy smile at her compliments on his work, his eyes aglow with pleasure as he showed his guests outside into his courtyard where he worked on much larger pieces in marble, alabaster, stone and fine woods. It had been arranged that Ella would visit each day to study with the old man and in the meantime, an easel, oil paints, and brushes had been delivered to the studio where she was staying. She was capable of holding a brush and Chen Lo considered it exercise for the hand and mind.

Chen Lo and Adam believed her ability, her spatial concept, was in her head and in time she would sculpt again. Ella explained that she was as she put it essentially a builder in clay and would not know how to proceed with a block of stone.

"When asked how he would sculpt an elephant Rodin replied that he would start with a very large block of stone and remove everything that is not an elephant." Was the reply of the old artisan.

"It's beautiful," Adam said from behind Ella's shoulder as she stood back to survey the finished canvas.

A study of a nude female, her back arched, head thrown back at such an angle the face was obscured lost in the shadows of the dark sepia background, the only points visible the bared throat and jawline. The shoulders and breasts were thrust forward, the legs were drawn up and thighs slightly apart. It was a wonderful depiction of a woman in the throes of an orgasm. The skin tones were perfect; the breasts had a translucency that enabled the fine blue veining to show through. Adam felt he could have touched the erect nipples, he felt his own erection stirring in his groin. The painting was incredibly erotic only the chiaroscuro effect of the shadows hiding all but the breasts saved it from becoming pure pornography.

She turned startled by his presence, not realizing that he had been watching in silence for a while.

"I feel exhausted, but it's a good feeling a little like I used to feel when I'd finished a piece of sculpture." She smiled and took the glass of wine he held out to her.

Adam tried to stem his growing tumescence and his hand trembled a little as he reached out a cloth in hand, "you've a little paint on your nose," he wiped it away and for a moment their eyes stayed fixed on one another's. He bent his head and kissed her mouth gently until he felt her respond with a quickening of her pulse but as the kiss grew more urgent Ella drew away.

"I'm sorry."

"No, don't be Adam, I'm not. It's time. But I want to talk to you. I miss my son Adam, I miss my life."

"There have been more reports of sightings of you in the press, it's still too dangerous, its _____"

"I want to go home, it's time."

Chapter Seventy Four

"Since that night, the opening night of the exhibition, I think I have been in a thick fog, a fugue state. The accident, Crystal's death___" she paused and swallowed audibly, a look of pain skittered across her face. "I will never get over Crystal's death Adam, at first I couldn't think beyond my grief, it seemed that was all that there was as though a pall of pain and loss had descended on me it blocked everything out. I don't think I even remembered the accident itself. Chen Lo was right being here has helped tremendously what do they call it getting in touch with your chi, being here doing the Taijiquan has brought focus back into my life the clouds have finally begun to drift away and I've begun to see all that happened. At first, the images were vague but while I have been painting I have had the stirrings of an idea. The sculpture that was stolen hasn't been recovered yet has it?"

"No, the police figure that Warrender has it, they were tipped off apparently by a Japanese guy, he's a millionaire, a collector, he told them that Warrender offered him the sculpture but of course there is no physical evidence. Warrender is being watched constantly but without that sculpture, they have little evidence to connect him to the guy who came after you or the two who died in the fire in the warehouse who they are certain were responsible for Crystal's death. They were known associates of Warrender but without the evidence, their case is stymied. So what is the idea?"

"Adam, Warrender is a buyer and seller, a fence, there is someone else behind all of this, the end buyer for want of a better word. Believe it or not, before all this happened I was always a pretty astute person, a good judge of character. Now that the fog is clearing I've been thinking about the opening night, the people there, the buyers, I even think I know, in fact, I'm fairly certain that I was introduced to whoever is doing this. I know who tipped them off, for instance, Hiro Takana; he was perhaps the only person there that I felt any empathy with. He told me about his only child dying of leukemia and we talked about loss and grief he must have informed because he knew of Crystal's death. But back to the collectors, its greed that fuels them Adam, the desire to own something that no one else does and one of them is a shark with the rapacity of a great white in a feeding frenzy."

"You haven't talked about any of this till now."

"I couldn't. It's as though I have been in a dark forest, blinded___I want to talk to Warrender."

"What?"

"I want Warrender to give this buyer whoever he is a message. The police think that Crystal's sculpture is the only one of any significance out there, am I right?"

"Yes, but I'm not sure where you're going with this."

"The sculpture is porcelain Adam; it was cast in Jian Arts factory by my own staff." Ella gave a little smile as she watched Adam's mind go through the machinations and the full implications of her statement dawn on him and a laugh exploded from his mouth.

"Wow!"

Ella leaned into Adam and he held her close, burying her head in his chest, stroking her hair gently. She was so precious to him this woman, he kissed the top of her head and she looked up at him and smiled.

"Take me to bed," she whispered.

Chapter Seventy Five

Ella stood before Adam in the bedroom her fingers fumbled slightly as she undid the buttons of his shirt, pressed her lips to his chest. She folded the shirt flaps back and began to trace her tongue down, across the nipples, down to the thin line of dark hair leading into his loose trousers. She knelt peeling them across his hips, teased his erect penis with her tongue until desire overcame him and winding his fingers into her thick hair he pulled her head forward and thrust himself into her mouth.

The urge to ejaculate pulsed through him and he drew himself away, pulling her mouth back to his own and smothering her lips with hard kisses, he lifted her to the bed. He tore at the front fastened shift dress popping the buttons easily, she wore no bra and in turn, he took each of her firm breasts, grazing the nipples with his teeth as he slid his fingers between her thighs and into her moist heat. His tongue tasted her sweetness and she raised her hips to him as the tidal wave of her orgasm washed over her and she moaned, "Now, please, now."

Ella watched him as he slept, did he love her, did she love him? She didn't know and he had not said, she was grateful for that. Crystal's death was a defining event in both their lives. No matter that they tried to put it behind them it still encroached on them and she wondered if they would ever be free of its shadow. Her fingers traced the defined muscles of his chest, lingering in the dark curled hair she felt him stir and grow hard against her thigh.

Chapter Seventy Six

It was almost midnight, Warrender was tired, he carried his brandy over to the window in his Mews house, only one table lamp and the fire dying in the hearth provided dim light behind him as he drew back the heavy velvet drape at the corner and peered out into the narrow street. The faint orange glow of the street lights reflected on the wet cobblestones and the dark outline of the unmarked police car. He thought he could discern the silhouettes of the two officers watching his house. The surveillance had slackened off lately; he sipped from the brandy bowl let the curtain fall back into place and went back to his cozy wing-backed chair by the fire. The newspaper lay folded, a picture of Ella Michaels playing with a panda cub uppermost, on the side table beneath the lamp. More reports of sightings of Ella Michaels, Cauldwell will want to move soon he thought smiling to himself when the phone beside him trilled unexpectedly.

"Hello?" Warrender answered cautiously, who would call him at this time of night?

"Mr. Warrender?"

"Yes, who is this?"

"Mr. Warrender, this is Ella Michaels."

"What? ____ " he was stunned, flabbergasted.

"This is a secure line Mr. Warrender, you need not worry, no one is taping this conversation, at least from my end, you can speak freely. I am calling to give you a message Mr. Warrender, one that you should pass on to your buyer." Ella's tone was pleasant almost friendly.

Warrender remained silent even now not wanting to commit himself, she had said they weren't being taped but he didn't trust that information and his phone may well be bugged at his end, he was unsure of just what could be used in evidence.

"Mr. Warrender I know who you are and I know that you were responsible for my daughter's death and the theft of the sculpture from her home. Have you considered at all that the sculpture you stole is made of porcelain; do you have any idea as to the process of manufacture of such a piece? When I make just such a sculpture as this I work in clay, this is a large piece and the firing process requires that no air whatsoever be trapped in the clay otherwise the piece would implode in the kiln. To prevent this happening and to lessen the weight to some degree when the clay is almost dry a mold is taken. When that mold in turn is dry, liquid porcelain is poured into the mold. After a short time, a mere couple of minutes really the mold is drained and what remains is a thin skin of porcelain inside. It is this skin that is fired in the kiln. The firing process takes little time, overnight in fact. Are you following me so far Mr. Warrender?"

"Go on Miss Michaels."

"You may also be aware that I own a manufacturing plant for porcelain and if not you should be now. When I made that sculpture, in particular, the one you murdered my daughter for, and the clay was ready, in what we ceramists refer to as the leather stage, a mold was made. That mold, Mr. Warrender is in my factory and later today I intend to instruct my son to commence pouring and in a couple of week's time, we will flood the market. I shall make unlimited copies of the sculpture available at a very low price; to me, it will be a fitting tribute to the memory of my daughter, who is of course depicted in the work.

When this has happened Mr. Warrender, considering your client's penchant for rarity and his willingness to kill for it, I doubt very much that you will live long enough to enjoy whatever ill-gotten gains you may have made. I'll leave you to consider that thought, goodnight Mr. Warrender."

There was a click and only the silence of the ether came from the phone still held in Warrender's hand. He stared at the phone, dumbstruck. Oh fuck, you clever bitch he thought. He poured himself another brandy and downed it in one, still shaking his head in disbelief. It had all been for nothing, he would tell Cauldwell of course it was a good job he hadn't sold him the sculpture yet and he was not foolish enough to try to cheat such a man. Tomorrow would suffice he thought as he went up the narrow stairs to his bed.

Chapter Seventy Seven

At the same time that Warrender had been listening to Ella Michaels destroy any illusions he may have had as to gaining financially from this debacle Max Cauldwell tossed the same paper with the news item of further sightings of Ella Michaels onto the desk in his study. The Tong's man had reported that she was studying with an old sculptor, and using the injured arm a little. He was tired of waiting. It was now or never, he decided.

At 2 a.m. in the morning, one of the two police officers sitting in their unmarked car outside Warrender's Chelsea Mews yawned listening to the sonorous sound of his partner sleeping beside him, looked up at the dark house, shuffled down in his seat and closed his eyes too. Neither of them heard a sound as the black-clad figures of two men wearing ski masks slid past them, down the dark narrow ginnel which separated this cottage from the one next door, through the unlocked gate and into the small rear courtyard of the house. Their entry was easy; Warrender had felt no need for the security of locks or alarms with the police sitting on his doorstep.

He was alone in his bed, sleeping, spread like a starfish across the silk cover. He awoke with a start as gloved fingers dug into his cheeks forcing his mouth open, a balled piece of rag was stuffed into it and tied in place at the back of his head. He was dragged naked and squealing into the bathroom and forced to sit down on the lavatory. The sudden glare of the fluorescent light blinded him, triggered a nauseating pain behind his eyes making him dazed and confused and he thrashed about wildly until the heavy blow of the pistol's grip split his cheekbone under his eye and momentarily stunned him. His head spun, and pain hammered like blacksmiths at an anvil inside his skull.

The men worked in silence, handcuffing his feet together at the ankles and taped his arms tight to his sides with strong packing tape immobilizing him. Tears mixed with the blood running down his face, snot streamed from his nose, his eyes were darting everywhere as he tried to speak, his pleading mere mumbled sounds indecipherable to his unknown assailants. There was little need for the restraints abject terror held him in a vice as one of the men removed his ski masks, Warreender knew in that instant, that he was going to die. The man took secateurs, a claw hammer, and a drill from a bag. In the small corner of his tormented brain that was barely still capable of lucid thought, Warrender smiled, knowing Cauldwell for all his efforts would never get what he wanted.

"Mr. Cauldwell thought this might be appropriate in a way." Warrender's head jerked violently from side to side as they lifted one hand and splayed out the fingers. One of them fixed the blades of the secateurs just above the knuckle of the index finger and with a crunch of bone cut clean through. Searing pain tore through Warrender's hand and arm and the blackness that shrouded him in a dead faint would have been a welcome relief had he been capable of conscious thought.

It was 10.30 a.m. in Beijing as the Tong's man crouched behind a low wall on a rooftop overlooking the courtyard of the old sculptor. His rifle rested on a tripod, its dull barrel had a silencer attached and he watched Ella Michaels through the crosshairs of I'ts telescopic lens, she was listening intently as the sculptor chiseled at a beautiful piece of Maple wood. The assassin's index finger sat lightly on the trigger as he waited patiently for the signal text to flash on the screen of his mobile.

"Now then, I'm going to remove the gag, no screaming now. We just want a little information then we'll go on our way."

The finger lay, pale, like an uncooked chipolata sausage in a bright pool of scarlet blood, on the virginal white tiled floor the nouveau cuisine of a demented chef. Warrender vomited, his stomach lurching violently almost spilling its contents on the shoes of one of his torturers, who jumped back laughing as he avoided the projectile. A loud wet explosion echoed around the porcelain bowl as he defecated and the bathroom was filled with the miasma of blood, vomit, and feces. The man coiled his fingers tightly in Warrender's hair and jerked his head back savagely.

Warrender's throat was raw, his breathing ragged and choked with the phlegm from his tears, he blinked rapidly as he tried to clear his jumbled thoughts their anchor of sanity torn adrift by pain. "I'll tell you___ what you want to know, just___ stop." Warrender gasped.

"Okay, where's the sculpture?"

Warrender gagged on the taste of his own bile and the dry cloth, retched again several times, the dry heaves tearing at his stomach muscles, filling his chest with agony. In his pain-wracked mind he knew holding back the information would only bring more torture, so he stammered out the address of the old lock-up. He had thought the code in exchange for money would keep him alive and satisfy Cauldwell long enough for him to get away. After Michaels call that was no longer an option, there was no need to even take the sculpture. Desperately he tried to form the words, to tell them that the crate was wired, they were no longer listening, but speaking on a mobile phone which one of them kept pressed to his ear.

Two men waited in a black van just a few streets away. The address received they sped away into the night.

"We'll just wait now, if your lying, well_____" He lifted the battery-powered drill and pressed his finger to the trigger, it whirred to life fully charged. Warrender's imagination conjured up the depths of pain to come and engulfed him in a blitz of sensory overload, his utter terror was excruciating and his mind slid down into gelid darkness that smothered all hope but one,

"Wait___wait, get Cauldwell, let me___let me speak to him."

"Begging isn't going to do you any good matey."

"You___you don't understand, please let me speak to him."

The wheels crunched on grit as the black van pulled alongside the lock-up under the railway arches. The occupants alighted and one of them approached the doors bolt cutters ready he popped the padlock and entered groping along the wall for the light switch. In the stark light of a single bulb, he spotted the wooden crate in the center of the brick-walled room and went quickly towards it. As he grasped one end of the crate, calling to his mate to hurry and help, a loud ticking filled the room. Bemused he turned the crate and saw the red LED numerals flashing their countdown.

"Holy fucking shit," he shouted turning and stumbling as he ran for the door.

The blast blew the doors across the street along with a sticky red mist of body parts. His mate was thrown back and slammed in a blackened and scorched pile against the still rocking black van. He lifted the open phone to his peeling lips.

"Fucking hell," he yelled, "it was booby-trapped; he blew the fucking thing up, Phil's dead, blown to bloody pieces."

Warrender heard the exchange and the bathroom filled with his hysterical laughter echoing off the tiles. His torturer spoke to Cauldwell. Through his growing hysteria, Warrender blurted out that Michaels had rung him, tried to form the right words to pluck them from his reeling unraveling mind.

"What is he saying?" demanded Cauldwell impatiently, "Why is he laughing like crazy?"

"Something about there being a mold and flooding the market, says a woman rang him."

"Ella Michaels, Ella Michaels rang me," screamed Warrender.

"Is he saying there are copies of this sculpture?"

"Yes, yes___all pointless___going to put them____going to sell them, Ella Michaels," his voice trailed off, his head sagged onto his chest, his shoulders shuddered with crying, and he voided his bowels again.

"Kill him."

The man flipped closed the phone, fitted the silencer to the gun hauled Warrender's head up by his hair and staring into his red tormented orbs pointed the gun. 'Phffftt'. A dark black hole appeared between Warrender's eyes, the light went out of them and the pristine tiles behind his head were sprayed scarlet.

Max Cauldwell threw the mobile phone across the room cursing, Peters skittered after it, and his back to Cauldwell he allowed his thin lips the slight twist of a smile. Peters had liked Ella Michaels at first sight.

In Beijing, the Tong's man read the message that flashed on the phone screen, eased his finger off the trigger and packed away the gun.

Ella Michaels and Adam Fergusson never knew just how close they had been to death on that morning and two days later returned to England.

Chapter Seventy Eight

Mihailovna stared down at the naked young woman lying amidst the tousled silk sheets; she didn't even remember her name, Shirley, Shelly, Sheila, fucking something or other. The bedroom had the fishy tang of female sex and stale marijuana buts lay in the ashtray beside the bed, a vivid pink phallus strap-on lay discarded on the carpet, her lips curled in distaste and she read again the small notification in the newspaper. Gaffy marched downstairs to the study where her secretary was working.

"Get her out of here and have the room cleaned thoroughly."

Later that evening she still held the paper as she sat staring at the magnificent bronze bust of her own image and as always was plagued by the memory of Ella working in her studio, her easy smile, her hands moving over the wet clay. Looking into the mirror as she poured herself another Absolut she watched as tears flowed down her now more hollow cheeks from eyes sunk deeper into her skull than those of the bronze, it was no longer a true reflection. Ella's laughing face along with her own, a blow-up of one of the few photos taken of them together, this one from the Garden Club, hung on one wall, happy, they had been happy then. The photo had come to light after the accident; there was a gleam, warmth, love in Ella's eyes, she could see it now why not then? a frozen image to forever haunt her. She teetered back to the sofa carrying the cordless phone and yet another shot of Absolut.

"I know you're back, I just want to talk, please, please let me speak to you. I'm still here, in England, I can't leave, just talk to me. The papers say you're better___that you're working again. Is that true? I do hope it's true. I'm coaching, English kids; you'd appreciate that wouldn't you____"

Ella listened to the slightly slurred voice until it trailed away in a sob and felt her heart clench in her chest, she turned to Adam.

"Where is she?"

"Jazz says he delivered the bust to somewhere in Eastbourne she told him she bought a house there, where you first met." Fergusson sighed he had feared this might happen but maybe it was for the best.

"Find me the address Adam please."

Chapter Seventy Nine

Even though she had learned that Warrender was dead and that it was suspected that the explosion had had some bearing on matters, fire and arson experts had reported finding pieces of porcelain in the debris, Ella still suffered bouts of paranoia, she still feared the wrath of Cauldwell and was occasionally frozen by the dread that someone was following her, watching her every move, she still never traveled alone, though this time she left the bodyguard and driver in the car as she mounted the steps to the elegant porticoed front door of the large detached Georgian house and rang the bell listening as it tinkled inside. The door was opened by Mihailovna's secretary.

"Oh my God, come in. I'm sorry please wait; um let me tell her___she'll want___"

"It's okay, I'll wait."

Mihailovna had washed the sweat off herself residue from a heavy workout designed to dispel the alcohol from her system, hurriedly pulled on a silk shirt and trousers; she glanced again into the mirror, straightened her hair again and tugged at the shirt trying to still her trembling hands her breath coming in small gasps, okay she thought, okay this is what I wanted, I can do this.

The happiness in Mihailovna's face was so palpable so powerful in its emotional impact Ella wanted to reach out but she knew that if she did she would be utterly undone.

Ella stood before her wearing a linen Armani suit, rumpled from the journey, and hanging on a slightly more emaciated frame than Gaffy remembered, yet she was still hauntingly beautiful.

"I asked them to destroy that," she said nodding in the direction of the bronze sculpture.

Gaffy moved towards Ella her arms outstretched in greeting, Ella backed off.

"I, I have stayed here, hoping____"

"You can't really believe that anything could be the same for us, that I could forget what happened?"

"I was angry Ella when you didn't come to Wimbledon, wouldn't speak when our last meeting had been an unresolved argument, I couldn't believe that I could be as stupid as to fall in love with someone straight, I felt as though you had just toyed with me."

"I was never without my kinks Gaffy. And Jana?"

"Jana?" Gaffy laughed dryly, "I pursued her, made her my own creature, why? Ego? Revenge? More likely for the same reason a dog licks its' own balls because I could. I should have waited, you came after all."

"A little longer perhaps, I was too late."

"I've been waiting now, I am your prisoner now Ella, this is my prison here where we first met, I'll go on waiting until you…"

Ella interrupted, "You shouldn't wait too long, I won't come again. Don't destroy your life."

"What like my stupid ego destroyed your's, Ella?"

"Did you destroy my life? Hm! I don't know I thought I was free, but I was my own prisoner Gaffy you merely forced me into a confrontation with myself. I tried to kill you."

"No. You were just angry. You lost that freedom because of me, all my fault," pain wrenched at Mihailovna, tears filling her eyes blurring her vision, "please Ella, don't hate me, forgive me, please I love you, I've never felt___"

Again Ella interrupted, "that was not my greatest loss Gaffy, that I could have overcome and the loss of my sculptures, maybe, well I have, the hand works in a fashion, but Crystal___my punishment for the events of that night, the loss of someone I loved. I don't hate you, maybe I did for a short time, but hate is difficult to hold onto. I grieve for my daughter, for you. I'm learning to live with it." Her voice trailed off and she shook her head resignedly; the stinging salty tears in her eyes lay unshed

Gaffy looked into Ella's eyes, "Joy once told me you were you were hard, made of steel."

"Perhaps I am Gaffy, it comes from a long way back, I'm a survivor and I could never have survived you in my life.

I am not angry anymore, I can forgive you for your part in all of this if that is all you need from me, but forget___no," Ella paused, "I came because I needed to know, to know what I felt, what you Americans call closure I think.

I loved you Gaffy. I was naïve, unsure. I have spent a good deal of time thinking since you called me a closet gay, I think now that maybe you are right but I'll never test the water, never dip my toe into that pool again. I would have done___was going to."

"Ella please, please don't walk away from me___I'm nothing, nothing without you in my life."

"It's too late. No Gaffy, compassion is all that I feel now."

Mihailovna sank to her knees remorse folding her in upon herself as Ella turned to shroud her tears of regret and left the house and Agafina Mihailovna forever.

Back at her house, Ella looked around her and sighed deeply, "In the words of an old song Adam, 'home is made for coming from and dreams of going to, which with any luck will never come true'.

"What song is that?"

"Oh, Lee Marvin, Wandering Star. I guess that maybe that's me now."

"I never realized you were such a film buff."

"I'm not but I like the lyrics to some songs, poetry to music really. Songs are so evocative we all remember what we were doing when a certain song is played." She smiled and sipped from her glass.

He reached out and kissed her hand, folding it inside his own. "Do the scars not bother you?" She asked.

"No, my love, nothing about you bothers me, least of all this, it's a beautiful hand."

He drew her up from the sofa, "we'll talk about it in bed."

THE AFTERMATH

Chapter Eighty

Fergusson had collected Jazz and Joy from the airport in Paphos, they marveled at their first sight of the island as the road, lined with pink and red oleanders the Mediterranean sparkling in the sun through the rear windows, rose high into the clear mountain air. The winter rains had turned the foothills into a patchwork cloak of lush spring greenery and carpets of pale lilac almond blossoms. As the road cut a pathway through high white rock chasms and traversed deep gorges and valleys Joy commented that if this was your first sight in a morning she could understand why Ella or anyone would choose to come here to live.

Later they sat on the patio in the golden glow of the last of the early evening sunlight. The pink-brown earth contrasted with the yellowing rough grasses, cinnamon gorse and the dozens of shades of grey and white striated rocks of the surrounding hills. A riot of colors, deep vermillion bougainvillea, violet ipomoeas, the lilac clustered blossoms of jacarandas and wisteria were trailing the old stone walls of the courtyard. The tips of the grey-green olive leaves, silvered by the dying light of the sun swayed lightly in the breeze.

The house had undergone considerable rebuilding and additions since the fire damage caused by Packer. A large swimming pool adorned with the sculptures from Ella's house and stone pillars found here on the island replicated the one in Lincolnshire and a state of the art fully-stocked painting studio and workshop, built in the local stone, the north side a glass wall, leading onto a small enclosed courtyard where Adam had erected an overhead boom system that powered stone cutting and polishing tools, were the most recognizable.

"So Warrender is dead and from what the police will tell me, not a good death, he was tortured they think to reveal where the sculpture was, which he did, but that they suspect was blown up in an explosion not far from where he lived on the same night that he died. There were traces of porcelain. They traced the lock-up back to him eventually but when they found him he was not a pretty sight. I feel no pity for him; my sister was a beautiful person she didn't deserve to die. They are still looking for Packer that was his name you know? Matt is doing okay, he and Xenon are living in my mother's house, Matt couldn't live where Crystal had died."

"Do you think they will ever find this Packer?' asked Joy.

"No, they'll never find him," Adam answered with surety.

"Elly is looking better, she seems to have lost some of that haunted look she had back in England. Some of the pain has gone from her eyes.

The paintings are wonderful too; they have a tremendous three-dimensional quality and I'm intrigued by their eroticism. I did though notice some rather harrowing ones in the studio." Joy referred mainly to the painting of a once white, innocent-looking door, now peeling, cracked and blistering with corruption. Ella had painted the screaming image of an emaciated child behind the glazed panel but had done something extraordinary with the glaze so that the figure could only be seen from certain angles. The painting entitled Behind Closed Doors, reminded Joy of Edvard Munch's The Scream and had the same jarring quality as images from a violent crime scene that nauseated yet fascinated in conjunction.

"Those are personal, not for a show I think they have been rather cathartic for Ella."

"She isn't sculpting though?" Jazz asked sadly.

"She has done a few pieces. Ella feels she has lost that particular sensitivity of her fingertips, the nuances of touch that allowed her to produce what she did. Chen Lo did a remarkable job, but not all the nerve endings have been restored. We have encouraged her to work with tools on wood and stone she felt clumsy with them at first but practice makes perfect or so they say.

This place is good for her; she asked me if she could be here, it was where she wanted to be, not that she needed to ask. I think she still felt vulnerable back at home in England, she had panic attacks was drinking a wee bit too much, couldn't think straight, if she stopped thinking of Crystal for a moment, stopped grieving, then she felt disloyal to her, disloyal to forget even for a moment that she was gone and certainly couldn't work and that she needed to do more than anything else." For a tacit man, it was a lengthy speech.

"And you Adam are you happy."

"I'm content, I exist on the periphery of Ella's world, I respect her space and her silences and she allows me to. I hope she is learning to trust me and if that day ever comes I shall be here."

"Is that enough to live on Elly's crumbs?"

"Aye, it's enough; a crumb from Ella is a good as a loaf from another." He laughed at his own aphorism.

"Does she ever mention Mihailovna?"

"Only the once, she saw her you know? Your mother loved Mihailovna, would have given all of herself to her but Mihailovna betrayed her trust, for once in her life Ella allowed herself a glimpse over the walls in which she had imprisoned herself and I doubt she'll take another peek for a long time, if ever."

"What about yourself Joy, no Ao."

"We're having a break." She answered lightly. "I think she's playing the field a bit for the moment. "She wants a child and me I'm, well I'm too busy with my career."

He paused reflectively then continued in a happier vein, "And right now I see Phillipos going into the studio, the sun's over the yardarm folks. I'll get Joseph to fix some drinks, about now Ella likes a vodka and tonic and I'm sure she'll be wanting to join us for a couple and fair dying to see yous and ha'e a wee puff of her homegrown."

The doors to the studio were open to a light afternoon breeze, a welcome relief from the heat of the day and young Phillipos knocked lightly before entering.

"Good afternoon Madam Ella, you are looking very beautiful today."

"Good afternoon Phillipos, and thank you for the thought though perhaps too much Zivania has tainted your vision."

The exchange was in Greek but Phillipos who prided himself on his ability continued in his slow but perfectly enunciated English, nodding at the painting of a majestic Mouflon standing proud on an outcropping of rock, which was drying on the large easel.

"I will pay 200 Cyprus pounds for this painting."

"300" answered Ella.

"Why this is too much, 250 and no more. I am your best customer is that not true and I am good publicity I show others that they should buy also?"

"275 and that is my final price Phillipos."

"It is ready now?"

"Tomorrow it will be dry."

"Okay, tomorrow I will bring the money; you are a good businesswoman Madam Ella. When will you paint me?" Phillipos said with a rare smile indicating some of the canvases of nudes propped against the studio walls.

"One-day Phillipos, when I am painting a Greek god."

"Do you think I am handsome?"

Ella regarded Phillipos. She was aware that with few young women in the village for Phillipos to choose from he occasionally saw her as a woman albeit one much too old for his years, though he had a grudging admiration for her. He smiled, when he volunteered one, with his whole face, showing gleaming white even teeth, his thick muscled arms and thighs were to Ella a mere visual illustration of his solidity. He was a rock and someday some young woman would realize just how dependable and worthy he was.

"Yes, Phillipos I do" she answered.

"You sold him another one?" asked Adam entering the studio and watching the retreating Phillipos as he climbed aboard his tractor. Fergusson had brought a tray on which two large vodka and tonics sat perspiring in the heat, he shook his head and laughed heartily. Ella's paintings already fetched thousands of pounds in England and America yet she constantly allowed Phillipos his small victories in their barter. Ella smiled recognizing the reason for Adam's laughter though she doubted that Adam recognized her reasoning. It had nothing to do with charity but with more to do with gratitude.

Galataria had recognized Ella, knew her for who she was beneath the polished urbane exterior, that she possessed that same ability they had, not that of a soldier, like Fergusson, trained to kill, but that malignity of an animal who when she or her pack was threatened would fight to survive to keep the status quo. She felt in part that she should be punished for taking a life but rationality told her it was foolish to consider that any form of physical punishment would do anything to assuage the guilt.

Galataria had embraced Ella but treated her with no more deference than any other member of their community and she, in turn, had embraced Galataria and folded herself inside the security of its'

cloak of anonymity. Painting scenes of traditional Cyprus was for her

a way of expressing some measure of the peace that she had found

there and the villagers had little interest in the rather more erotic

nudes that had become known to the rest of the world as Ella's style.

Joy was alone on the patio when Ella came silently behind her,

resting her hands on Joy's shoulders, her fingers smoothing Joy's

wayward curls.

"How are you really, without Ao I mean?"

Joy turned and for a second Ella's face seemed to morph into

Gaffy's, then the image skittered away and was gone, she gasped as

Ella leaned in and kissed her. It was a more intimate kiss than Ella

had ever given before and she wondered if she too would always be

grateful for scattered crumbs.

EPILOGUE

Chapter Eighty One

Stephan Mickiewicz was in the kitchen, he carefully wiped down the stainless steel sink for the fourth time, a slight drip fell from the tap and splatted on the shiny surface, he cursed then went outside to the back yard and retrieved his toolbox from the shed. Coming back inside he dismantled the tap and replaced the washer, putting the tools back in their correct slots in the box. He wiped the sink again and stood for ten minutes watching the tap until he was certain, wiped the sink again and carefully folded the dishcloth, corner to corner and placed it in the small plastic container fitting the lid down tight. He lined the container, the washing up liquid and the hand wash exactly parallel to the edge of the sink. When he was satisfied he scanned the kitchen a final time, checked the cupboard where the food tins were, all the labels were facing outwards, he wiped away an imaginary speck of dust closed the door and rode the Stanna stair lift up to one of the bedrooms he used as a studio. He had installed it for his mother but he had psoriatic arthritis which was distorting his hands and feet especially, the doctor's treated him for gout, but he knew what it really was, either way, it was painful and the lift came in handy.

The house was ex-council property, a corner plot; making it a semi-detached four bedrooms with a sizeable front garden, which he kept immaculate. He had lived in the house with his mother for many years until her death. Over time he had spent a good deal of his income, putting in the new kitchen and having it decorated of course, he had added molded plaster covings, well that is to say he had brought professional decorators in to do the job but when he had continually pointed out the errors they had walked off refusing to work for him. The same was true of the council workmen, they refused to visit the house after a while, no one likes to be told their job by a better man he thought. Of course, the council had caused a problem at one time when they had only rented the house, it was too big for two people they said and they wanted it back for a family, he and his mother should be moved to a small bungalow. Stephan didn't like change and his mother was too old to be moving, anyway,

Gabriella had solved that little problem, she had bought the house for her mother on Maggie Thatcher's' right to buy scheme.

God! That had been a turn up for the book, a solicitor coming in the day after the funeral and dropping a bombshell, he laughed to himself remembering the look of shock on the faces of his sisters and their husbands, those that still managed to have one that is. They were in the process of a massive argument as to how he would have to move and the house be sold, the proceeds shared out amongst them when the solicitor had calmly informed them that technically the house belonged to Gabriella. She was canny Gabriella she must have anticipated exactly this happening, the vultures gathering for the feast. He chuckled again remembering the scene that had ensued, it seemed the house had been gifted to Stephan for his lifetime it was his home after all said the solicitor and afterward was to pass to a nephew Gavin who had some mental problems; he was a paranoid schizophrenic, not surprising in this family thought Stephan.

From the shelf, he took down a large leather book. The cover was beautiful workmanship, the leather had been painstakingly tooled and hand-painted, in the center was a portrait of Gabriella, or Ella, as she called herself these days, and surrounding the oval picture were exquisitely rendered freesias, Gabriella's favorite flowers, his mother had told him when he had asked, she loved the perfume, but only white ones now, she didn't like the bright colors. He started at the beginning as he always did, looking over each page, of surreptitiously collected photos, some pages contained copies of poems she had written when she was younger, meticulously copied out in Old English Script, which Stephan had bought special broad tipped pens for, each page a work of art in itself styled on the old bibles the monks had inscribed, he had even treated the paper, washing it with cold tea, dropping the odd grain of granulated coffee on them and scorching the edges here and there. Graduation photos and later ones of the kids followed, Crystal and Jazz, great kids thought Stephan, nothing like the rest of his nephews and nieces who by and large he had little or no time for, he doubted Gabriella knew that her children had contact with him, small but a couple of times a year they visited. He loved that Jazz, stupid name though, a solid dependable bloke that and clever too, he usually sorted out Stephan's computer when he visited. Gabriella had done a great job with them, she was right to keep them away from this family. He wiped a tear from his eye as his gnarled arthritic hand caressed the photo of Crystal, a law unto herself that one like her mother before her.

He moved slowly through the pages, through the news reports from when she had had the factory and the reception for the Chinese there, not surprising she had fled there in the end. He lingered over the brochures for the exhibition and a collection of photos taken by him.

God what a nightmare that day had been for him, the careful planning, all the routes drawn out, the train and tube timetables, and his inner fears tumbling round inside his head but he had made it, his only ever trip to London. Stephan had sat on a bench in the gallery containing Gabriella's work for two hours, he wasn't a bad painter and drawer, but this, this was art, he had stared lovingly at the sculptures even imagined he saw a little of himself in one or two. He had been admiring one in particular when the stranger spoke to him.

"Beautiful aren't they?"

"Aye that they are."

"Terrible what's been happening to the artist, the death of her daughter and having to hide. She must be quite a person to produce these."

"Aye, she is."

"You sound as though you know her personally."

"That I do, she's my little sister."

The stranger's eyebrows had risen in surprise and not a little disbelief until Stephan took out his wallet and showed him several photos of Ella, as a child and as an adult there was no mistaking who they were.

"Actually, she looks rather like you."

"Aye, spitting image, not that she'd be pleased if you told her that. Well, nice talking to you," and with that Stephan had hobbled away, leaning hard on his walking stick and grimacing with the pain, but his heart was swollen with pride.

Stephan scanned the latest news clipping through his machine, he didn't use the actual newspaper, he considered the quality too poor for his purposes, but had bought top grade paper. He lined up the scanned sheet on the cutting board, plucked the scalpel from among the other lined up tools and pencils and drawing paraphernalia and using the metal ruler trimmed the document precisely. With the finest sable brushes, he painted the signature freesia in the lower right corner and waited patiently for it to dry before meticulously placing it against the marks which lined up the dead center of the page.

In the dimness of his memory, he saw her again as the scrawny little kid, she'd always had guts he had to give her that, if she'd only stayed down when he punched her, but no she had to get up again and stand up to him, she'd even spat in his face once, and there was the time she had almost bashed his skull in with the poker, she had balls Gabriella, more than any man he'd ever met.

He closed the scrapbook and placed it carefully back on the shelf making sure the edges lined up exactly, took down one of his many Mensa puzzle books and turned to the rest of his daily routine and his solitude his visit with Gabriella had been a little longer today than usual. He set the timer on the stopwatch the better to check the speed of his answers.